So Close to Murder

Sabena Burnett

Cover Illustration by Rory Burnett

*Lovingly dedicated to
Marc Burnett*

Contents

Chapter 1: Excess Baggage – 7

Chapter 2: Overdose – 23

Chapter 3: Burglars on the Roof – 47

Chapter 4: Pop goes the Weasel – 61

Chapter 5: Fast Eddie – 83

Chapter 6: Bad Rubbish – 93

Chapter 7: The Guv'nor – 109

Chapter 8: Dead Pool – 121

Chapter 9: Builder's Bum – 133

Chapter 10: Why Rocky? - 143

Chapter 11 The End of the Road, or is it? - 157

Chapter 12 Is this Justice? - 170

Chapter 13 So Close to Murder – 183

Chapter 1 Excess Baggage

Shakira and Rocky Browning's departure from North London was incredibly dramatic. When Rocky witnessed the gang murder on the already lawless estate, it changed their lives forever. For some while the gang had lurked around the place looking for a victim, their demeanour exuding violence. These were damaged young people who had time on their hands, and a penchant for trouble. Even before the fall out of this particular murder erupted, they had given the impression it may not have been their first atrocity, and that it was unlikely to be their last.

Rocky had seen the whole episode, from the sharpness of the first knife piercing the skin. He watched the disbelief as the image of horror was reflected on the face of Rocky's neighbour Carl, It was an image that was forever etched on his soul.

Carl who was sitting on the ground below Rocky's window, held on tightly on to what was left of the lad he barely knew although he lived so nearby. Now his life force was spilling out onto Carl's arms and on to the pavement.

Usually burning with curiosity Shakira, found herself emotionally exhausted by the nightly caterwauling that seeped carnage into the dark sky. She could hear them orchestrating another monstrosity, so physically close to where her children were sleeping. She did not even wish to be a spectator to the latest heinous event and shied away from any vision of the latest outrage. After a while the unspoken trauma on Rocky's face drew Shakira to look out at what had disturbed him so.

Only feet from where she stood at the window she saw what troubled him. Carl was nurturing the young victim. So much of his fresh blood was on the concrete that it reflected in the street-lamps.

Rocky told her he needed to go and help, now that the last of baying wolves had dissipated. They kept hearing the ambulance approaching the estate from different places unable to negotiate the maze of anti-joyriding barriers. The architects appeared to have forgotten real people might need to live here.

It was a long time before Rocky was able to explain to Shakira the full nightmare of what he saw that warm evening. To be able to explain what, was causing him to wake up in a cold sweat, screaming with such fear that it frightened his children. As for Carl, he never really recovered from the tragedy.

Rocky told her,
"It was that dreadful smell, not just the familiar faint whiff of blood, but an overwhelming stench that you could not escape. It was everything, blood, shit, piss, vomit and anything else you can think of, all of it at once. Then there was that noise. The rattling gurgling sound the lad was making, trying to breathe through his own gore. When Carl turned him over gently to stop him drowning, we knew he was gone. We watched him powerlessly as the soul fell out of his eyes."

She understood that having the misfortune to watch, while someone's existence is needlessly extinguished, changes your entire aspect on the perception of life's value.

Despite recognising that Rocky was still struggling to comprehend the awfulness, the police soon picked up on his credibility and intelligence. They soon realised Rocky's testimony would be imperative to the conviction of perpetrators of this dreadful crime.
They were painfully aware that most of the estate's inhabitants were addled with drugs and drink, or bound and gagged by their own previous convictions. These factors also made them susceptible to the intimidation by a gang who knew everything about them necessary for intimidation.

Rocky was a newcomer, a fresh face and despite the 'us and them' attitude of the local law, they recognised Rocky's sense of morality would make him much easier to lead to the witness box.

Naively Rocky and Shakira believed the Met when they promised to protect them and keep them all safe. Despite the gang's blatant and visible threats to assassinate of the whole family, it soon became apparent that the 'specialist' detectives, were almost hostile. Even before they got Rocky to the Old Bailey, they wavered between incompetence and a worryingly cavalier attitude to other people's mortality. Due to the imminent danger and being dropped like hot coals after the trial by the very institution that was supposed to protect them, Shakira and Rocky moved themselves to Norwich because Shakira had family nearby.

It was years later and in the comparative safety of their new home that Rocky and Shakira discovered their phone was being tapped. They immediately saw this intrusion as part of the Mets continual and desperate quest to find them guilty of something. At the time one of their protectors had illustrated the attitude perfectly, even before they had escaped the urban clutches of the inner city.

"Oh come on everyone who lived on that estate was up to something."

Under these circumstances you would think Shakira might have been put off the judicial system. Especially with regard to her roots in the arse end of London where everyone was expected to mistrust the 'filth' anyway. Surprisingly she still believed in the thin blue line whatever its shortcomings and that law enforcement was the last resistance for the survival of many of the vulnerable people in the city she had left behind. Particularly as she had often been amongst their number herself. As much as she would be regarded as a pretty unlikely candidate, Shakira's secret goal was to be a detective.

At least ten years into their imposed settlement into the complete cultural contrast that was Norwich and way after they had earned the obligatory 'passport' that was eventually awarded to incomers into the community that she had worked so hard making herself an integral part of, Shakira took early redundancy. Her career as a Housing Officer had been unremarkable and it was the right time to follow her real ambition. She had taken up an opportunity for a degree in Police Management, with the Institute of Criminology which naturally culminated in an internship. After a short interview she arrived at Wymondham Police Station, or officially Norfolk Constabulary Force Headquarters, to work under the guidance of Detective Chief Inspector Arthur Hunter.

Arthur's bite was not as bad as his bark and she was able to allay her initial feelings of fear and isolation, in the knowledge that she was not the only 'outsider' in the gaff. There was a whole civilian section on the R.A.C.E. (Research of Accidental and Cold Enquiries) project that Arthur had found himself landed with, under guise of 'joined-up justice' or whatever they called it this week. Although floating amongst the crocodiles in the same boat, they couldn't help using their little clique mentality to treat Shakira with a certain distain.
The vast, state of the art Police Station, designed to serve the entire county was situated, bizarrely, in an unobtrusive small Norfolk town, miles from the city, and distant from much criminal activity.
Arthur was also the team's SIO. He cut an imposing figure in his well-tailored suit, even by constabulary standards. Even as he introduced himself to her, he made it obvious that he only tolerated post-graduates under protest because one of his higher echelons thought it looked good for business.

He told Shakira, "I come from the old school of arrest, interrogate and bang-up. As far as I am concerned any namby-pamby snowflake attitude, has no place in proper coppering."
He may have typified Norfolk man in some respects, but he was certainly not of the forelock touching breed.

"What about rehabilitation of offenders Chief Inspector?" Shakira enquired, blatantly challenging his ethos from the get-go, despite a nagging insecurity in her knowledge of the protocol of her new role.
"I leave all that to the CPS. The local hooligans can be rehabilitated after they've been banged up". He retorted smirking at his own irony.

She may have just left college, but she brought with her a vast experience of dealing with the local populous, criminal or otherwise. Years of earning respect in the vicinity made her feel that this insular community's rank and file inspired little enthusiasm and displayed even less ability. Especially her old adversary Jonathan, whose disinterest in the unfortunates he was supposed to help had got up her nose in the Housing Dept.

Wherever she was, he kept turning up like a bad penny. She decided to ignore him and concentrate on learning from the real professionals, namely the police and probation officers. When she felt their objections putting her under pressure, she would take a deep breath, a moment to look outside at the beautiful countryside and calm down while counting her blessings.

She returned home to report one day's events to Rocky, and scathingly mentioned working with the dreaded Jonathan again. Rocky became incensed having thought they had successfully shaken off this millstone round their necks. Now Jonathan was stuck under their feet again, like a dog turd.

Rocky had also experienced the misfortune of working with this idling appendage and unable to help himself, he ranted,

"That tosser! I went out of my way to get him a job, because he was so 'desperate' and then he went out of his way to persuade the boss to get rid of me. I don't want to interfere with your work, Shakira but I would keep away from that two faced twat wherever possible!"

Shakira nodded in agreement,
"While he was back in the office holding forth about his wonderful rapport with homeless people because of his expertise in housing, I had been busy out in the field sorting out the mess he'd left behind. His customers used to threaten violence if they were sent back to him"
They both shook their heads in disbelief and giggled.

Shakira had met Rocky a decade ago, in a music pub in London not far from where she was born. She was introduced to the place by one of her many friends in the music industry, Adam King, lead singer of King's Men, a band whose roots hailed from Nottingham. Shakira's accent may have been unmistakably London, but her looks betrayed a lineage nearer Dhaka than Dalston.

Rocky's dialect was more difficult to place. Only very occasionally did his brogue betray his seldom mentioned roots, or upbringing in the shadow of The Potteries. Any way he had more of an affinity with Nottingham, where he still had friends from his University days. Shakira's visits with the band had made the city her second home. In fact Rocky and Shakira had often moved in the same circles even before they met. They had only been together a short while when they realised Shakira had a brief liaison with a guitarist in London, years before he and Rocky became best mates in Nottingham.

Rocky liked London too. He had lived there for ten years before meeting Shakira so the sudden move meant he missed the place. Shakira on the other hand had left a whole lifetime behind, and even after putting so much effort into her family's new home, she still often yearned to be back there, bathing in that quagmire of stormy waters where history was made. After the immediate danger had subsided they did return occasionally, but the once indelible ink of their London story, began to fade, and the incident which changed their lives so dramatically became a distant memory. Shakira could not entirely let go, so she kept in touch with her former buddies online.

A little mindful about security given her job and previous circumstances, when she begun getting some weird messages online, she consulted her colleagues. They brushed it off by saying anonymous trolls were rife, but they did advise her to report anything that was of particular concern, so she contemplated the possible source of just where this unwanted communication had come from.

Long before meeting Rocky, and way before he witnessed the murder, in point of fact, the reason she got stuck in the urban ghetto in the first place, was to shake off her violent, mentally unstable ex-husband, Adrian. She had only agreed to the council plonking her on the labyrinth-like barbarian estate so he could no-longer find her.

She had good reason to think he was responsible for the strange correspondence because in an attempt to stop her leaving him, he had threatened to commit suicide. Then he vowed to kill her and anyone else he could blame and he tried following her around thinking she would 'come to her senses'. He wouldn't be able to resist attempting some nasty retribution if he had stumbled upon some method of contact.
"Some people just require more detergent to wash off your skin than others." She told a colleague.

Then there was Rocky's violent ex-partner who had also left an indelible mark, her attempts at stabbing him while he was asleep and at his most vulnerable had caused him to 'sleep with one eye opened' as they say.
She told herself that both these monsters were confined to the annals of history, buried somewhere in the archives of time. Adrian was probably in the company of the estate boys in some prison by now. Accepting that some people are beyond help, she didn't give Adrian another thought.

To Shakira's delight, not long after her arrival, Arthur had called her into his office and announced,

"Tomorrow I would like you to move in here and start working with the police Shakira. You'll be looking into accidental deaths and suicides. If your research gives us enough proof that there has been an unsolved crime, we will use it to re-open the case. Therefore your work will be of the utmost importance."

He introduced her to Detective Inspector Julian Storm who was to be her mentor. She had studied his demeanour around the place. Like Arthur, people treated Julian Storm as though he might vanquish them at any moment, but she was not fazed by this. Her experience told her that many managers who found themselves surrounded by sycophants preferred her style of refreshing frankness. That seemed to be the case with Julian. Of course this did not stop her being wary of his Armani suited confidence. It had bestowed him the air of considerable accomplishment. The 'by the book' reputation he enjoyed was mainly perpetrated by his minions, and as a criticism it was probably undeserved. All that said, she soon warmed to his no nonsense approach.

Younger than Julian and Shakira, his assistant DS Michael Saint's male pattern baldness did nothing to detract from her observations. He displayed the demeanour of someone who would have been comfortable at a pop festival. However smart his suits and crisply ironed his shirts, he always looked slightly dishevelled. The laid back persona he sported, may have ingratiated the hoi polloi but it was a thin disguise, behind which was a profoundly experienced, efficient and intellectual policeman. He was more eloquent than his boss and often got him out of trouble. He was also a professional listener who sometimes hid behind the guise of being busy with something else, whilst actually solving the problem you had brought to him, albeit at the same time.

A liberal and modern thinker, Micky Saint's management style allowed Shakira's renegade methods more than a little leeway, provided she got results without treading on too many toes. This was in contrast to Julian and particularly Arthur, who often reminded her to keep a professional distance from the criminal element.

The preponderance that technically she was still a protected witness, alerted her to a possible cause of Arthur's treatment of her. Although an open secret among her close friends, she did not want the less well informed in her vicinity, returning to the 'London gangster who had turned turtle' theory. Even some of her more insular colleagues had pandered to this silly piece of gossip. Her inner need to elucidate on such a difficult period in her life had long since waned.

This, however, was not the case with Rocky who had never stopped subtly perpetuating the 'gangsta' myth. His sense of devilment often found him holding forth in the pub, resulting in their reputation as a pair of survivors who should not be messed with, which did them no harm.

Shakira liked the RACE team and she found police and probation officers, who liked to wallow in gallows humour, less stuffy than the civilians Tis was a survival necessity in what could be quite a morbid job. Taking the dramatic with a pinch of salt was imperative.

Then there were Diane and Liz, who had been leading lights in local community policing since time immemorial, and partners even longer. Their lives, both personal and professional seemed inextricably intertwined. Despite having entirely different body shapes, you could imagine them choosing clothes together, from the same catalogue. They had been assigned to supporting Rocky and Shakira when they first turned up as vulnerable and lost victims at their lowest ebb. The experience of being guided through this very personal trauma by these two experts in their field, although slightly embarrassing, had instilled trust in Shakira. Despite their nodding acquaintance with her domestic situation, they were a pleasure to work with.

Before long she had been allowed out on a call. She found herself in the back of a police car taking notes, while Julian drove at 120 miles an hour he was barking a running commentary above the blues and twos. She observed interrogations and Becky promised to tutor her in the complexities of the Forensics Lab. Although not enamoured by firearms, she was particularly impressed with the in house, state of the art firing range, understanding this was a necessity in the tools of modern crime fighting. After all these were times of terrorist attacks and possible nuclear war. Later she was introduced to Nick Furn another intern who also preferred working the front line rather than watching endless power-point presentations. Like Shakira he advocated fighting the lawless with prevention and rehabilitation. Shakira and Nick got on well.

She found the other incumbents of the office were not so trustworthy. Sensing she was a little under-confident and self-conscious they began treating Shakira as if she was not only wet behind the ears, but needed wrapping in cotton wool. Under pressure and intending to illustrate her resilience and street wisdom she had unwisely related a story in the pub that caused her to remind herself to 'engage brain before opening gob'.

"A builder working opposite our house" she explained "had blocked the lane with his van. He ignored Rocky's polite request to move, and further incurred his wrath by arrogantly proclaiming that seeing as how he was born here he could park where he liked. Foolishly he attempted to resume a phone conversation in his hut which ended abruptly when I snatched the phone out of his hand and slammed it on the receiver whilst yelling "Now move your van!" or words to that effect.

"While visibly astonished at a woman who appeared to fear nothing, he looked up to encounter the much more fearsome and very handy figure of Rocky blatantly approaching the locked van with the intention of shifting it without use of the engine. When the fool picked up a monkey wrench ostensibly to threaten Rocky with, I quickly removed it from his grasp and handed it to Rocky who was now pursuing him for his van keys.

Rocky had forgotten he was still clutching the thing but the silly builder hadn't and it scared the living shit out of him. Slipping into the driver's seat he swiftly reversed out of the way before Rocky caught up with him.

Rocky drove me straight to work without mentioning the incident and we did not give it another thought. The next day, a new fella turned up on site. Later someone told us Mr. Van Man had been set upon in a local pub. Obviously Rocky and I were not his only adversaries!"

Instead of amusing her audience as she intended, Julian and Micky made a big old fuss in case she should bump into this numpty again, or he should recognise her driving her distinctive second hand Land Rover.

The anecdote backfired even more, when one afternoon she and Nick were watching one of Julian's interviews from an adjoining room, unaware that one of her ex-housing customers was also under interrogation close by.

Fred Fisher still blamed Shakira for his return to prison, assuming she had betrayed a confidence causing him to be breached. When she and Nick emerged from the room chatting, Freddie spotted her on his way to a cell and all hell broke loose. After a half-hearted death threat- hardly the first she'd ever encountered- he was dragged back into the room while she was shuffled out of his way.

Despite their reluctance to listen, she tried to inform the doubters that she was well acquainted with Freddie and that the bluster he exhibited in his soporific state would soon wear off, and he would calm down. In truth she was somewhat miffed at their unnecessary panic. Freddie was much more likely to listen to her that anyone else present, but the incident was used to demean her ability.

A couple of weeks later she bumped into him in the city. After his sullen greeting she seized the opportunity to tell him unreservedly but gently,

"I would never have betrayed anything you said to me in confidence. Whatever got you breached it did not come from me, even if you had confessed to murder, I am an intern not an informant, but I am sorry I yelled at you. I was put under pressure."

"What if I had confessed to murder then?" he challenged her

"I'd talk to you later, when the drugs wore off"

He laughed and although still not particularly cordial, it broke the ice with a subtle indication that he accepted her mitigation and just said,

"Alright, Shakira gotta go!"

She did not feel inclined to mention this somewhat tacit truce to anyone, as she felt any progress she had made with Freddie had already been sabotaged.

When later a nightclub bouncer warned her some chap had asked after her, in slightly sinister tones, she decided it sounded like one of Fred's baleful mumblings and thought no more about it. She'd had a belly full of the delicate flower treatment, so she had kept their chance encounter quiet. Even when she discovered Fred should have been at probation when she saw him, and Sgt Parker wanted a word with him about a burglary, she still kept it to herself.

Late on Friday Liz whispered discreetly,

"I've got a phone call for you. He won't give his name but I have a fair idea who it is."

When she picked up the phone it was Fred. She quietly pointed out that despite her keeping shtum, he was deep in the doodoo. He was yelling from somewhere noisy,

"Look I'm on ringing from a payphone. I just wanted to see my missus and kids before I get sent down again." He moaned.

"You know you are making things worse for yourself, Fred. Oh alright I'll have a word with Sgt Parker and see if he'll give you until Monday. I don't know what his answer will be but I can try" she said persuasively.

"What if I don't turn-up?" he said pushing his luck.

"I'll send them round to Sheila's. I don't suppose you've got a phone on you by any chance?"

"Alright, go and talk to old Nosy for me. Promise him I'll be at the nearest nick, first thing Monday. I'll ring you back in an hour"

His response told her it had been a good guess. She related some of this to Rod Parker who said,

"You know where the bugger is don't you Shakira!"

"I could make an educated guess" she replied "and more importantly he *thinks* I know. If he's not in your custody early doors I will give you the benefit of my education. The odds are better than chasing him round the countryside"

"If it all goes on the wonk, I'll be coming to see your boss. Oh go on then, tell the little varmin Monday morning or I won't just be chucking the book at him, I'll be slinging the whole bloody library!" He conceded ungraciously.

Freddie rang back but had no more change. Shakira just had time to warn him "I *will* bloody grass on you this time if you are not in custody by lunchtime Monday."

He said "Thanks Shakira" it was the nicest the arsy little sod had ever been to her.

On Monday morning Shakira waited at Norwich station and caught sight of him as he came off the 8.50 from Yarmouth. She told him to get in and drove him to Bethel Street as it opened.

Micky told Shakira,

"You put yourself at risk with Freddie, you should have told us you were going to fetch him, nevertheless it was a fierce bit of ol' quality constabulary, Shakira", he pronounced it constaboolery.

"If I had told you would have started this cotton woolly stuff again and sent some muscle to protect me" she said sarcastically,

"Yes, true I suppose I probably might have sent Liz or Diane" he retorted with a chuckle.

"What a waste of resource that would have been", she retaliated, ignoring his little jest "we both know they have far more important work than dealing with the likes of Freddie Fisher".

As she left the room she heard Micky say,

"I know she is a bit wild, I'll have to rein her in a bit"

Julian quipped "Rein her in, you'll have to put her on a bloody leash boy!"

If they had seen her slinging tooled up brawny nutters out of nightclubs in London, they would know she found keeping the average Norfolk felon out of trouble was pedestrian to her, and she wasn't talking traffic division. She was however still excited by the prospect of changing the world for the better, as part of the Norfolk Constaboolary.

Chapter 2 Overdose

Shakira's take on The Larkman had always been that it had its problems. Most of them were caused by negligence of one sort or another, with a fair smattering of abject poverty. The place hardly equated with the 'murder mile' reputation of her old stomping ground. Unlike the two-story coffins that masqueraded as social housing in overcrowded London, these dwellings were proper living spaces. The brick built terraces many of them pebble-dashed and whitewashed, may have been a little regimented, but they did help to retain some of the close community ties, reminiscent of the villages of old Norfolk. That said, a death by overdose there, even that of a known addict was still a fairly unremarkable event.

Shakira had been entrusted with her first cold-case assignment. The Coroner's Report which had listed the death as 'accidental, drug related' was so non descriptive it was almost obstructive. The fact that it lacked the inclusion of words like suicide, manslaughter or even murder, led her to assume that none of these had been ruled out. These omissions gave it a nasty pong of 'who cares.' This lack of interest in such a short wasted life suggested to her the possibility that there was almost something arcane about her cohort's reaction to this urban tragedy. Like an itch they were not told not to scratch.

"I suppose an open verdict would have required far too much graft but nobody's death should be taken this lightly", she muttered to herself, although she was perfectly well aware that all Class A's were rife, even in this quietish backwater. Maybe Arthur sensed something else was awry and hoped Shakira would uncover a little gem to restore his faith in humanity, or at least next year's budget.

Initially she needed to unearth the vendor who had sold smack to a hopeless heroin addict like Jonah. At first she thought it may had been cut with something lethal. So rather than ask to go further up the command chain, she tactfully approached First Officer Attending.

The FOA, was cagey and wanted Arthur's approval before spilling any beans. Under a shroud of secrecy, and acting as if her interest made her some kind of infidel, she was able eventually able to extract a vital detail.

"Even at the scene we were able to ascertain the gear was pure 'China White' Shakira"

"Oh. I *see*" she responded throwing her eyes in the air and relieving him of the necessity to embark on the rigmarole surrounding the issue. She had become painfully aware of the effects of this unusually strong heroin in London. The trouble with scag that lacked in profit enhancing additives, was that addicts mainlined their usual amount, which caused overdose. Its primary source as far as she understood was still China Town logically, as China was its country of origin. Not prevalent in Norwich just yet, she knew any influx had to be kept out of the press and nipped in the bud. The FAO continued,

"Needless to say Jonah's neighbours could not shed any light on where he might have got his drugs from, in fact once they worked out who was asking, they suddenly had amnesia about knowing him at all. Under such circumstances they were surprisingly forthcoming about his penchant for propping up the bar at The Dog and Trumpet."

She expressed her gratitude for his little snippet and plotted her next move. As it was unlikely she could sneak into this den of iniquity without some miscreant recognising her, she started her quest elsewhere.

First of all she must work out how the offending product had found its way to this part of sleepy Norfolk. None of the First Responders could shed any light and sneaking about in the CCTV room might be an issue. She had determined that establishing the source would put her one step ahead of the game and more importantly, the might of County Lines and The NCA. Possible interference in that direction made her reluctant to furnish her colleagues with her strategy, until she had results with substance to present. She emailed Micky with some guff about having some course work to finish the next day.

Having signed out a '*company* car' the day before because Rocky had needed to use the Land Rover, she had concerns that her secret mission would have been compromised by payment of the congestion charge. So she stopped at a mate's flat before approaching the area. For a moment she assumed her clandestine movements had been rumbled as a blue BMW kept appearing in her mirror, often the sort of vehicle favoured by detectives. But as she turned into the alley behind her pal's flat, it disappeared. Omitting to mention that the shiny Audi she had hidden in his tatty garage belonged to The Babylon, she took the 73 into Oxford Street.

This bus route gave her a strange feeling of deja vu as she passed some of her old haunts. Having made her way to The Dutch Tar, a pub on the outskirts of China Town, she wondered if too much time had elapsed for her to blend in with the regulars, as none of the clientele looked familiar. Of course there was the expected collection of mainly Chinese gamblers playing a noisy game of Mah-Jong in a back room.

Just as she begun to think about heading back to Highbury, the door of the crowded and lively pub opened and she saw a face she recognised. Fortunately the ex-policeman turned security guard also remembered her. As a freelance copper's nark his grapevine would have already established her as part of the firm so she trusted in his discretion. After some sketchy details of drug activity on the dreary estate, he confirmed that Soho was likely to have been the prime source of the offending chemical.

"The trouble is" he elucidated helpfully "the more dangerous the gear, the more attractive it is to your average smack-head. As you know red light districts have a huge captive audience so none of the small fry need to risk shifting it anywhere else."

"I can only think of a few players with the wherewithal to move it about, the most likely are a couple of hooligans from Nottingham." He went on to mention several contenders including a Darius. This name sounded somehow familiar to Shakira. The security guard went on to explain,

"I don't know Nottingham well, but I remember they chatted about a couple of tidy gaffes considered safe to do business in, the rest is your call." As he wrote a list of establishments on the back of a fag packet, he advised her,

"They'd move the product by courier, village to village, by push bike and moped, but Norwich is a long way, and Nottingham is probably further. Taking it by motor would be too easy for the 'county lines' lot to track, especially on the motorway. Amateurs might be thick enough to use something flash like a beamer with blacked out windows, but these ain't gonna be no amateurs." He laughed ominously.

She wanted to see if there was a connection between this Darius and Norwich first off, she felt sure there was.

It was getting dark when she posted the garage keys in her mate's letter box. As she drove back, she mulled over all the people she had left behind still living on the edge of existence. She thought she saw the beamer again for a split second, but when she looked back it was not there, so she decided she must have been mistaken.

Having found something to work on, she realised she would need to fess-up to Micky the real purpose of her journey to London. She had decided returning the car to the cop shop garage, before anyone arrived the next morning would be a good start. This task accomplished, and despite the risk, she popped in to The Dog to try and find out where Jonah copped his dodgy gear. Intelligence was likely to be her only mitigation to arm herself with, when she faced the inevitable music.

Even as early as eleven when the pub doors opened, not only were both the customers in this dilapidated dump stotious, but one of the horrible urchins was trying to chat her up. She decided to use his audacity to her best advantage, preferably without him slobbering all over her. So she spoke in her best 'junkie', slurring that she had been a good mate of Jonah's. The best the urchin could muster in an attempt to commiserate was,

"I wan't too surprised though, he'd got really bad. Last week he was trying to score off some northern chap and he managed to get wrong with him. Next minute they were thacking lumps out of each other. When the coppers turned up, I heard them yelling at him,

"You'll now be going back to Norwich, then boy!" I knew Jonah was on the wonk. He couldn't even score, without cocking it up."

When he fell silent, Shakira thought it was best to escape, before he sobered up and regretted his little chat with a complete stranger. More to the point, she did not want to encounter Darius or any other of Norwich's nasties just yet.

After lunch she told Micky the truth about her little jaunt, but didn't mention The Dog. He began formally,

"I know you like to use your initiative, but you must do it within the boundaries of…." He interrupted his own reprimand suddenly by squealing,

"Hold you hard, my woman. I know this dealer from Nottingham, he was arrested and banged up last week for breach of probation"

He got straight on the computer and verified his assertion,

"Darius Bradshaw. I'm sure I've heard that name somewhere else, but I can't remember where"

With a glint in her eye and sensing that his heart wasn't in the bollocking anyway, she intervened cheekily,

"Consider my wrist duly slapped! Look I've got a mate in Nottingham that knows so much gossip they call him The Evening Post after the local paper. But I *can* trust him to keep his gob shut if I ask him to, can I go and talk to him?"

"Yes, but not on your own" he said, meaning not without him, and at the minute we are up to our ears in it.

Later Shakira told Rocky she had permission to investigate someone in Nottingham. Guessing that she had ignored any word of caution from Micky, Rocky reasoned,

"Before you consider hastily tearing up there this weekend, in order to chip away at some little mystery and into god knows what, let's have a bit of concern for your own safety. Much as I admire your capabilities and don't want to interfere, just let me accompany you on this one occasion as soon as I have found someone to look after the sprogs."

Pretending to admit defeat, she smiled in agreement.

"Of course only if Mr Plod says I'm allowed!" he added sarcastically and then he added, still tongue in cheek,

"You could always tell Micky I'm an expert in Nottingham's underworld"

"I don't think that would help somehow, darlin'" she responded.

Against his better judgement Micky agreed she could go to Nottingham with Rocky as minder. She convinced him that Rocky's familiarity with Nottingham would come in handy and she had watched 'Kings Men' play in all the local dives so she knew the runners and riders.

Rocky, liked being her chaperone, especially when it was an excuse to bump into the aforementioned underworld who were likely to be wobbling about in any of these watering holes, especially a music pub called The Greyhound.

On second thoughts a low profile would be best, so he steered her round the corner to The Eagle instead, a pub far too boring to be on her list.

However, he did hope to discover their mate Kenny nailed to the same stool he had been parked on last time they had visited the pub. That meeting had given Kenny a bit of a jolt. Two people he had been close to, separately and in different cities, arrived together and unannounced in his favourite watering hole, virtually on his doorstep. Not only that, without his permission they had met, got married and had kids.

So this time they were a tad disappointed and perhaps a little concerned when Kenny was not in The Eagle. They were advised he had done one of his disappearing acts about a year ago. When America was mentioned it made a little more sense, as many of her muso friends had gone over to do some gigs and decided to stay there.

"He never said a word on Facebook" she whispered to Rocky "mind you he disappeared from London when he'd made enough enemies, and popped up back here".

Still it was Bernie she had come to see and she did not want to make it too obvious, so she nodded at Rocky and he made the sort of phone call that precedes buying some weed. Shakira slithered off her stool in the direction of Bernie's house and left Rocky 'holding court'.

Despite Bernie managing to avoid actually meeting this low-life, she was not surprised that he had an in-depth knowledge of Darius's shenanigans,

"You will need to be careful of that one, me duck", he said "dangerous with a munk on he is. If coppers get a sniff that he had 'owt to do with Norwich. Darius would come looking for yah. Your youth was waiting for him in The Greyhound once. I buggered off before he turned up and haven't been back"

"Jonah?" she asked,

"Yep, that was him, sounded like he'd lost his village, kept mithering about Darius making him take all the risk moving the gear. They tell me Darius has got some other wassock who can't drive trundling gear on the train to Norwich now. If someone was flogging nasty scag it'd most likely be Darius"

Shakira told Bernie it was probably best if she did not hang around for both their sakes. She thanked him for his tea and information and went to rescue Rocky from the pub. When she got there, she realised she had become designated driver for the return journey.

Rocky had got bored and started on the lager and then added the whisky. He slurred an apology in her direction and then some farewells as he wobbled in the direction of the car to go back home. On the way back after a short sleep had sobered him up, he asked if she got what she wanted.

"Yes thanks darlin', oh and Bernie says hello," she answered vaguely because she thought she spotted that blue beamer in the rear view mirror again, but decided this Darius geezer was making her paranoid. On that note she added,

"I'll need to keep Bernie out of it. I am glad you were with me because this particular pharmacist sounds a right nasty piece of work. I presume he's still indoors, not that any of my dopey lot would have told me if he had been released, Bernie has managed to avoid him so far, so I doubt he'll find out we've been here." She was wrong about this.

The next day Micky was still snowed under. So she bashed out an outline of the day's events and emailed him some juicy morsels but with very little detail. When she did catch up with him, he was somewhat formal while a little blasé.

"Yes Shakira" he muttered "your day out was quite interesting, sometime we'll have to look into this Darius chap". She had not mentioned Bernie by name and Micky did not ask. She was irked by his dismissive attitude, especially as she had risked her neck to gain some pertinent titbits on something she had been asked to work on, which Micky seemed to suddenly find unimportant.

To add insult to injury, Julian came in with a motorway accident for her to look into. He did not ask where she had been. She expected Micky had squared it with him, but thought discretion might be a good idea in case she put her foot in it. Patronised by this mundane task and with her abilities clearly still under scrutiny, she was determined to prove she was good at this detecting lark.

As he had left some drivel in the notes about knowing the victim, she felt compelled to consult the dreaded Jonathan. As she approached his vacant desk, she plonked a 'post it' on his computer, causing his colleague Fiona to grunt without looking up,

"He's *is* still off sick you know!"

Not wanting to reveal her annoyance at the assumption that she would be party to the dopey dollop's whereabouts Shakira asked politely,

"Perhaps *you* could help me? I'm working on traffic accident ..." before Shakira could finish Fiona said scathingly,

"As *I* did not know any of *that lot* personally I can't help you". Undeterred by her uncalled for animosity Shakira persisted,

"Will he be in tomorrow do you think?"

"I'm surprised *you* hadn't heard he's in hospital after the attack outside the pub"

"Oh?" said Shakira, not playing her 'everyone must know the office gossip,' game asked,

"Has he been mugged or something?" said Shakira

"Well I'm not at liberty to tell *you* if you have not been spoken to."

Fiona whispered mysteriously to the dreary woman next to her, as if his plight was somehow Shakira's fault. As she was not interested enough in Jonathan's welfare to start playing twenty questions, she left the room and muttered,

"I'll wait until he's better then thanks!"

Fortunately Jonathan's input was superfluous to a solution. His ailment remained part of the usual subterfuge the populous of his part of the station seemed to think enhanced their importance.

"Perhaps it was an STD" she told Rocky sniggering.

"Must have encountered one of your more desperate crims then," he added smirking naughtily.

Her accident was presumed to be a hit and run, and as there were no witnesses Shakira did not take this as read. The post mortem seemed very vague, but established the cause of death as a heart attack. The elderly man had blatantly been knocked off his feet, and Becky's crew had briefly attended the crash scene. Shakira used this as an excuse to ring her. Becky started pouring forth immediately,

"There were two anomalies, hang on a moment I'll be right with you,"

Shakira was pleasantly surprised when she came straight to her desk. It may have been her cut glass accent, but Shakira had previously found Becky a little frosty, so she wanted an opportunity to get her onside. As if continuing the sentence she had started on the phone she went on,

"a lack of any debris from the car like glass or plastic or skid marks"

"Couldn't that be more to do with an anti-lock braking system, than failure to stop though?" Shakira interjected intelligently. "Sorry what was the other one?"

"He had only superficial injuries from the collision." Almost as if her reply was obvious, Shakira continued,

"So the vehicle was travelling at low speed and hardly touched him. Supposing the driver was already pulling out of this lay-by" she conjectured pointing at her diagram

"He would be looking at the oncoming traffic. The old fella probably appeared out of the bushes and walked into his blind spot as he moved out. He may not have realised they had made contact. Then if he collapsed because of the shock of being hit, rather than as a result of minor abrasions, that would catch the driver's eye enough for him to stop."

"Surely the gentleman would have told him if he was hurt?" Becky surmised,

"Not the stubborn old buggers round here, especially if it he thought he was at fault. Even if he was asked, he probably made out he was fine out of embarrassment." She replied

"But the driver should have reported it, especially if he had passed out"

"Perhaps he didn't pass out, perhaps he fell over when the car made contact and the driver picked him up and dusted him down, and perhaps the man insisted he was uninjured and sent the driver packing."

Becky did not interrupt her conjecture. Erroneously Shakira took that as a sign of approval and carried on,

"Especially if he threatened to ring an ambulance, you know how some elderly people hate a fuss. If the driver left assuming he was OK, he could have gone into shock afterwards, then had the heart attack. A driver in any of those scenarios, might not think of it as a hit and run or see a necessity to come forward even if, technically, they should have done"

"Far too much 'perhaps' for my liking, but I suppose we could have another at the coat" she said over her shoulder as she flounced out of the room.

Shakira had not been aware, but her theory was tangible enough to irk Becky who saw questioning her conclusions as being a little forthcoming, even arrogant. Absolutely the opposite of Shakira's intention, but running with it nevertheless, Becky looked again at some trace evidence on the man's coat including some mud from a fall. A partial print on his button matched prints that were on the system.

When Micky spoke to him, the driver had no idea he had hit the old boy and he helped him up just as Shakira surmised. He assured Micky he didn't leave the old boy until he looked fine, so he was distressed to find out he had died. However, he was relieved when he was exonerated by Micky because of the forensics. It never occurred to Shakira that Becky should have deduced it was an accident herself.

After a couple of weeks, Micky suddenly said nonchalantly "As designated detective looking into this Darius chap, I would like to invite you to come to Nottingham and take notes for me. Of course you will have to manage without your husband, Shakira, but your initial research was a fierce bit of constabulary by the way" he chuckled.

"It would seem your northern bloke who Jonah had a bit of a spat with in The Cat *was* the same Darius. The same pair were shouting about Nottingham, before they had another punch up in The Butchers Arms, so we'll need to talk to the landlord who slung them out".

Sean was a manager to whom multitasking was seamless. As they watched, he signed some delivery man's clip board, while also serving the old fella wearing a white suit and a bowling cap, while ordering a particular real ale on his computer having consulted his barman and he threw food orders over his shoulder in the direction of the chef. He would have answered their questions at the same time had it been politic. It wasn't, so he subtly ushered them on to the jetty next to the river with a promise of some dappled sunshine, and spoke in dulcet tones. He had remembered the fight well,

"They came over from Bethel Street, pretty fast!" he said, "I was serving upstairs when the two idiots started going at it hammer and tongs in there" he said pointing indoors at a tiny room "smashing chairs and tables. I didn't hear any particular theme to the argument but some of my regulars might have heard the gist of the yelling. I'll find out and get back to you"

The next day when she drove Micky to Nottingham, he warned her,

"Much as I want to avoid involving him, I might need a quick chat with your mate at some point before I arrest this boil on the bum. We've got an ident, but I still need to prove he is directly responsible for Jonah's death".

"You think he caused him to OD on purpose don't you?" she asked

His silence response told her he did not want to proffer an opinion but that he had come to that conclusion too.

He changed the subject, "Do you know a guitarist called Jimi, I'm meeting him at a pub in Hyson Green".

"No but I know The King Lear well" She grinned knowing by his reaction she'd guessed the right place.

Indeed when they got there she didn't recognise Jimi. She plonked herself in a seat looking away from his conversation with a local DS but she was near enough to take notes. Micky came in later and introduced himself. Jimi began to explain

"I'm too well known at the Greyhound" He spluttered nervously looking around before he begun,

"Well Darius was having a right old bundle with some manky bloke who sounded like he'd just got off his tractor" Micky laughed, "His name was something from the bible"

"Jonah!" blurted Micky "and you mean he spoke like me?" he laughed,

"Yes, I think so" Jimi muttered, too busy trying to remember, to be embarrassed by his own description,

"They was *always* at it .Usually over drugs, money and some rammel about trains, and he kept running on about *his boys*, I thought he was a nonce at first, then I realised he meant runners. They had a row in here once. *He*," Jimi nodded towards the bar "threatened to ring you lot and told them to put a sock in it so off they went!"

On the way back Micky remarked in his best posh, "These two gentlemen were not very suited as partners in business"

"Or even in crime" quipped Shakira, only half listening, then she said more definitely,

"Trains! One of Sean's customers told him they argued over trains and Jimi referred to trains. Jonah didn't drive so he took the gear on the train, so the kids must pick it up from him. There is probably a bunch of spotty herberts hanging round the back of Norwich Station as we speak."

"Unless his new lackey drives of course" Micky mumbled "Nope, he doesn't" she said firmly.

As soon as they got back to the 'factory' as Shakira called it, Micky got a call from Sean. He paraphrased the conversation for Shakira, "Yep one of his locals said they kept yelling some squit about trains, and he told them the Northern bloke said he'd just come from the station"

Shakira joked "Apart from train spotting what's our next move?"

"Spotting characters who could have been cast in the film. Their star turn will be out next and we need to re-engage him for a part in Porridge" he said sternly.

Shakira was glad it was not sooner. There was a piece of her that did not want to bump into this purveyor of destruction, until she had recalled who the hell he was. Micky had shown her a mug-shot on his tablet. She knew the face well, but god knows from where. When she and Micky went to meet him in The Dog, he was eerily familiar, but why?

Micky approached him and asked him politely "Can we pop outside for a chat? I'm dying for a smoke"

He rolled Darius one as well. Shakira watched quietly from inside as instructed. From her seat by the window she could see both of them smoking rollys on the corner. After a quick conversation, Darius disappeared and Micky came round to the pub door and beckoned her towards the car.

As they returned to the station Micky explained,

"Darius denied ever visiting Soho and said he didn't know a Jonah, but had heard something about a bloke being found dead. He made out he was just staying with friends in Norwich for a couple of days to talk to someone about a job."

Shakira retorted "He seems to have a remarkable knowledge of the pubs hereabouts, for someone who had just popped down for a job interview. Must be looking for a position as a brewery sales rep!"

"Or perhaps he punts a nice line in pub furniture!" quipped Micky.

When she got home, Rocky had received a disturbing phone call. Roger, a friend of Bernie's rang to warn him that some maniac came in to The Eagle, kicking off about how he was looking for Bernie to batter him stupid. He told Roger,

"Tell your nark friend we know all about his visit from the filth. He had better keep away because when I catch up with him he'll wish kept his gob shut."

She knew it wasn't Darius as Roger had said he was Bengali. Fortunately, this would be assailant didn't know his home address or his favourite pub, which certainly wasn't The Eagle. When she told Julian, she had decided it was for the best, he castigated her and then insisted,

"You'd better keep your distance too, and keep away from The Dog, god knows what possessed you to go in there, and I don't want to catch you two near Nottingham. If you can warn your mate to lie low, without it ending up in The Sun, that would be useful. I'm afraid we will need to go and talk to him Shakira."

Then Arthur called Shakira to his office and gave her a right ear-bashing about her own safety. He pointed out "You are not officially supposed to be part of any investigation. Your remit was to observe and take notes for your thesis and that was it."

She went back to her desk very upset. She understood that she had often overstepped the mark, but Micky had sanctioned her last excursion. She thought for a while and then went to see Micky.

"Can I speak to you privately" she began in fluent 'shop steward' "I don't think you are being fair with me Micky, you approved my visit to see Bernie and I got some good intelligence. It was your decision to talk to Darius in The Dog and then when it all goes tits up you've got Arthur blaming me" Micky interrupted by putting his hand up to stop her and said,

"Hold you on, my girl before you put on your parts, Arthur's got his knickers in a knot about your welfare, I got wrong with him over it too, Arthur's nasty particular about safety. You don't even have the same insurance as the rest of us here and Darius is not the problem. You've got yourself a hacker, my woman and it's not him"

He picked up her phone and started scanning through it,

"A hacker on my own phone? Oh come on, what could they want to hack?" she mocked "Pictures of my dinner?"

"We know they have got into your Instagram which is a potential security breach!" He responded formally.

"That's clever of them, I'm not on Instagram." She muttered still not showing concern.

"You are now," he gave her back her phone but pointed at some pictures of her kids he'd accessed on his own phone.

"How the hell?" she trailed off. "I took those and I've never shared them with anyone, someone is playing silly buggers!"

"Maybe, but it could be serious", he replied gently "the IT boys are looking into it, but I suggest you encrypt everything. The likelihood is your Bluetooth was on, in a public place and they were in close enough proximity to pick them up. It's not your dopy ex either, they've shaken him down thoroughly"

"I hate technology!" she said after passing her phone back to Micky,

"Can you ask them to sort it out for me please Micky? She asked sheepishly,

By way of punishment she was given 'another bleedin' car crash' to look at.

Later Julian emerged from Arthur's office, looking pensive as if he'd had a rollicking as well. He told her softly,

"The Chief Super has made it clear you can only leave the office with Micky and you are not to go out on your own and don't take that bloody phone" He threw her a cheap mobile sporting a white sticker with the number scrawled on it.

"The Service Desk is going to re-whassit the whoosit on it for her!" Micky shouted after Julian as he left who muttered over his shoulder.

"I'm now going to see that code 4 witness before his Mum goes to work" and rushed out.

Later her curiosity got the better of her, Rocky was always teasing her about her nosiness, and how she'd always got her 'trunk' into everything.

Eventually she said "If Julian is talking to a minor what's the betting he was one of Darius' cuckoos" she reminded him "Probably based on the intel from *my* London nark", she said cockily hoping to persuade him,

Micky was not amused, biting his tongue he explained gravely,

"Before you go on let me show you the picture of you and Rocky at the Falcon that has just been posted on Instagram using the wifi at a pub in Thorpe called the Dragon. There is also a picture of your friend in the Eagle on the same date you were there. The friend that you told Julian was in America"

"That's weird, we never drink in The Dragon and the blokes in The Eagle implied he had moved to The US on a permanent basis. Maybe it was just a bunch of drunks playing a game" Then she said thoughtfully "That phone's driving me mental, Oh Christ what did Julian say?"

"He's still on the Larkman so I haven't mentioned it. Let's keep it that way."

When he came back, Julian explained,

"Last night front desk got a call from the greenskeeper at the Sportsground who was cleaning the floor. He had spotted some lads hanging around outside. One lad, who he knew, was being teased and called a 'saps'. He was the one I went to see this morning, he had taken a right hiding. Fearing for his own safety, the greenskeeper turned off the light so the place looked empty, and rang us. He didn't dare leave until they had all cleared off, even the attending officers did not give the game away."

With some intervention by his Mum this lad Damon had to come clean,

"I was supposed to meet a pal in Clover Hill on the edge of the Estate." Julian read from his notebook "Before I could talk to him, two blokes with their faces covered with scarves and hoodies jumped out from behind the football clubhouse and kicked seven bales out of me. My mate scarpered. They nicked my money, phone and everything and only stopped because the police came."

"He only knew the lad he went to see by his nick name, Lamb Shank. When I caught up with this other nuisance, he protested his innocence and tried to say he was just meeting Damon for a drink, and had nothing to do with the others.

Eventually this Damon admitted to associating with Darius's crew, but had been told he'd gone back to Nottingham. Drugs were not mentioned by either party, so I just took their statements and left it at that."

Arthur decided there was enough evidence to show Darius sold Jonah the gear that killed him, but not enough to prove culpability for his intentional death, yet. He submitted what he had to the CPS. Nottingham police executed a warrant to search his flat and were then able to hold Darius on charges of "Possession with Intent to Supply and Child Criminal Exploitation."

Julian ensured Shakira and Micky were completely out of the picture when they arrested Darius. At first he seemed to have resigned himself to the possibility of a stretch, he knew he would get custodial. What they didn't expect was his sudden rant as soon as he got out the pub. Amongst other ramblings he told anyone that would listen that,

"That Rocky will regret his mouth when he's in the morgue and that Shakira's a dead woman!"

Arthur was outraged when Darius was released on bail especially after his threats and the drugged up state he had been found in. It was not uncommon for the police to disagree with a judge, but Arthur's description of the decision included words he was seldom heard using and they certainly weren't in legalese.

Darius was allowed to go back to his flat in Nottingham where he was told to stay and they would pick him up and drive him to Norwich Crown Court the next day. However he slipped out in the evening and they could not find him. They had not panicked as they assumed he'd gone to score for himself and would be back soon, but it rang an alarm bells for Micky who was concerned about Shakira. He persuaded Arthur to sanction a helicopter which was able to track him, eventually to Jonah's old flat on the Larkman.

They were sure he was in there but it took a while for them to get a warrant and open the door with a big red key.

Darius still had the needle still in his arm. After the usual red-tape he was pronounced dead at the scene.

Chapter 3 Burglars on the Roof

Ethan lived in a remote cottage located in an unusually picturesque village, north of Norwich. It came with a large garden, featuring an orchard of huge Bramley apple trees that were so abundant, that the ground was always laden with fallen fruit. The situation was begging for a productive person to make something countrified with it like cider or chutney. The idyllic flint covered dwelling, may have been a little uncared for, but it overlooked nothing but farmland for miles. Ethan's landlord had attended a local school with his Dad, so his rent was nominal and much of the acreage belonged to his close neighbours who he trusted implicitly, so there was no lock on his cottage's back door.

At the back of his unkempt garden was an old brick potting shed from the days when it was an asparagus nursery, and where Ethan had previously grown a bit of weed. Now between the shed and the apple trees, you would find an assortment of push bikes in various states of disrepair, some under an old car port, and others in rows covered in large tarpaulins. Ethan's little cycle workshop was the cheapest place to get your bike fixed, or to buy a re-conditioned one that somebody had fallen out of love with. Ethan may have been on Mr. Plod's radar at one time, but these days he stuck to Old Holborn.

Ethan and Leila had been at school together and what she lacked in street wisdom, she made up for in loyalty. Leila used to pop round and cook for Ethan occasionally and sometimes she would just tidy a little without being intrusive. Although she was apt to wander in unannounced, if he was busy, especially with a woman, she would wander out again. He was like an older brother and very protective of her, especially when she took up with nerks like Jack. Him: Ethan was not so fond of!

So when, out of the blue, his humble abode was broken into, the culprit was quickly identified by a very short process of elimination. Jack's main source of income was hoisting, that is lifting/thieving goods to you and I. Ethan's missing articles were quick sales items and he recalled Leila foolishly once trotted the stroppy git through Ethan's back door, making it obvious it was always unlocked. But her old schoolmate naturally assumed the gypsy warning had been applied.

Now Ethan, was solid sort of chap, pretty tough. To the brighter inhabitants of Norfolk, he was hard enough not to be messed with, but soft enough to give you his last sandwich. His pal Nikos, along with his assorted cohorts who hailed from Essex, were a different story. They dabbled in many little businesses, from drug trafficking and dealing, to prostitution and armed bank robbery. Ethan was quite aware of this, but was sharp enough to know when to shut-up, so he was never a liability, and at least one of them owed him a favour.

Nikos, who hailed from Tottenham, although not originally, was charming with the shedloads of charisma required of a ruthless career criminal. Maybe unwisely, Ethan thought Jack's transgression was worthy of retribution. As Nikos was staying at his 'holiday home' in Thorpe End, Ethan had hatched a plan to bump into him whilst he partook of the local ale in his favourite hostelry, The Old Forge. Seeing Nikos in company he lurked surreptitiously at the bar until Nikos joined him out of curiosity, under the guise of purchasing a round. He discreetly related the gist of the recent obtrusion on his personality, and the name of the likely suspect, without creating attention from the hoi polloi.

He became aware that his subtle approach had been wasted. Ethan's assumption was that any reprisal would only be impacted towards the guilty party. This intention may have been lost in translation. He overheard a couple of Nikos's dolts reading out the address of Leila's flat rather than Jack's hovel. He begun to regret his reaction realising his desire for vengeance might have been a touch impetuous. Maybe Nikos had realised the mistake by now, or maybe not. Certainly Ethan had not wished to correct his operation at this late stage, and decided to leave it be.

After he had waited nervously in the pub and overheard the offending fool returning to report that the flat was empty, Nikos sensed Ethan's relief and that he regretted making a fuss. He enquired, and not gently,

"Where you think the ginnal gane to?"

Ethan just said cautiously "I'll let you know when I find the bastard".

"The ball in your court, blud, irie" whispered Nikos tactfully.

Presently, after a quick reccy, Ethan realised that the somewhat brighter of the pair of 'no neck monsters' had cottoned on to the obvious. That being that Jack had not lived at Leila's flat for a while, nor had he graced his own slum with a recent presence. Ethan's guessed that the relationship between useful but dopey Jack, and his ex- girlfriend Leila may have been rekindled, and this fact would not have escaped Nikos, either.

Although still seething, but having already made a bit of an arse of himself, Ethan thought he'd better put the whole situation on a back burner. After all Leila had previously told him she had dumped Jack, but her own absence gave him an uncomfortable feeling she had been culpable in some way. Later a mate put him straight on this, "Leila split up with Jack ages ago. Her Mum's been ill so she's probably round hers."

Still sceptical about whether Leila was aware of Jack's recent antics, he was in two minds about contacting her. In fact he was still unsettled by it all when, owing to Mum's better health, she came bouncing through his back door, apparently oblivious to recent events. To add insult to his injury her normally sharp eye missed the shiny new lock on the opened back door, not to mention the lack of recognition pertaining to his formidable carpentry skills. This did not deter him from elaborating on the injustice that had befallen him by yelling a lot of inaudible ravings as he followed her, ending with….

"I'll kill that Jack when I get hold of him, the thieving scum!"

She thought for a moment trying to work out the logic of his ramblings and then said cautiously,

"I might have plenty of good reasons to twat the brainless dork, but I can't imagine him being daft enough to risk you belting him. Jack would never be brave enough to do something to incur your wrath, especially not robbing your place, he wouldn't dare. Her protestations, which still dared to imply Jack had a set of morals, only served to irritate Ethan further. Especially as earlier one of his neighbours had described someone like Jack, up on the roof trying to get in Ethan's loft. The onlooker ended his observation with,

"I kept telling Leila he was a waste of space!"

After the old mates had several hours of discussion, and indulged in an excess of Jim Beam, Ethan's brain went into overload. The red mist took over and he grabbed hold of Leila putting an old kitchen knife to her throat, demanding an admission of guilt. Leila was having none of it and just laughed at him and protested,

"You know me better than this and *I* know you are not going to hurt me "she scoffed, "In fact I'm furious you would think I could be complicit in any of Jack's crap!"

Eventually he calmed down, especially as the truth dawned on her and she stopped standing up for Jack and promised to find the bugger. Much calmer now Ethan slurred, "I sent the boys round to find Jack, but they went round yours by mistake." He sniggered but she retaliated triumphantly, "It's a good job I was round me Mum's then, wasn't it!"

Leila knew 'the boys' would involve Nikos, and was now convinced Jack was the villain of the piece. She decided to find him herself before anyone got hurt. Jack was bound to have some woman in tow, he always did. This was why she had dumped him in the first place, making her emotions still a little raw. Realising he wouldn't go home because Merseyside coppers were looking for him, she worked out exactly where to locate this merry band of thieves. The bunch of losers, as she called them, would be languishing on the channel island of Jersey. The other 'losers' were his mate Derek, Derek's son Desmond and his pal Pascal. Still, she managed a smile while being particularly scathing about Jack's accomplices,

"None of them ever showed even a smattering of honour amongst thieves", she told Ethan, "they were all totally mercenary".

Derek was a clapped out alcoholic always looking for a mark to pay for his next drink. Jack was handsome and oozing machismo making women an easy target, so it was in Derek's interest to stick with him .The other two were just daft boys, who did not have the 'street' of the older men. The troupe's chaotic lifestyle, and nomadic existence left them all pretty insecure and rootless.

They had been tipped off that she was on the island and had skidaddled. Since she had come all this way to do him a favour by warning him, she was furious and emphatic. It was time to stop mollycoddling Jack and go home. Any consequences were self-inflicted.

Now more concerned about the repercussions on Ethan, she went to see her sensible mate Shakira. She related her tale while sipping tea in their living room, surrounded by the usual hectic hive of activity that children and their friends create.

"I can't go to the police" she said, "I'll be a target for the Southend mob".

Shakira said, "Surely if this Nikos is still fond of you, he can be persuaded to put a stop to the whole nonsense before it escalates."

Rocky disagreed, "I've heard about his lot from the bikers. *They* won't let *her* interfere with their business. I'm sorry Leila, I think Shakira should take some advice from her colleagues, she doesn't need to mention you by name!" After some persuasion, Leila agreed.

Micky was not familiar with this tribe of out of town villains, but he was confident in the accuracy of Rocky's street wisdom and wanted Leila's friend, who he had worked out was Ethan, to continue keeping his nose clean. At Rocky's suggestion, he went to scoop up some gossip from the bikers at The Old Forge. Even before finishing his first pint, he heard a local bumpkin embellishing his association with the gang. Rather than risk any discourse with the loud mouthed liability, he let him run on, while he asked the guvnor quietly if his friend Nikos still liked to drink there.

"You've just missed him", he replied adding cautiously "he went back today, but he might come in next week". Micky had heard enough.

Shakira had first met Leila at a King's Men gig and begun to wonder if the Southend hoodlums had any connection with the band. Adam, who was not unknown to the Essex underworld was the person to ask about Nikos. Ever cautious on the phone, he just indicated other musicians might know him better. He explained "One of the band had a trade with Nikos years ago" *Trade* meaning sexual relationship, "Just ask Rocky's mate Ethan, he knows him well"

Shakira had not mentioned Ethan's name and it was news to her that he and Rocky had ever met, so she gave him the third degree when she got home. He was very apologetic,

"I met him through the Roamers bike club", he explained

"I didn't mention him because I used to go round his to his buy weed, when he stopped doing it, he sold his motorbike and started his push-bike business", he said sheepishly, "in fact it was him who warned me about the Essex gang and some bloke called Nikos!"

Jack's exploits were old news to Micky, but he thought he had pushed his luck with this recent little venture. When Leila's Mum, Lily filled out a Missing Person's Report which landed on Julian's desk he was convinced. Lily had predicted Leila was,

"Lying in a ditch somewhere!"

Recently assured by the tech boys that her phone was sorted, Micky had requested that Shakira message her on Facebook privately in the hope she would respond. Instead, bizarrely, one of the King's Men messaged her to say news of Leila's disappearance had gone viral. Micky was livid. Shakira's work computer being compromised was serious. Later that day, a call came through to Micky's phone for Shakira. Keane from Oregon had heard Leila was missing from some random English muso in a local bar there. Micky took his number and checked it out before letting her return the call on the office phone.

Meanwhile fed-up with hiding out, Leila decided to risk talking to Nikos after-all. When she arrived in Essex, his missus Marie answered the door and said he was in Norfolk. She invited Leila to stay there until he returned and covertly texted Nikos.

Leila looked at her own phone and the text from Shakira. She contacted Lily straight away who didn't mention the police. Feeling a bit silly for panicking, Lily rang Micky to tell him Leila had been located.

By chance Shakira picked up Lily's call on Micky's line. She did not know Shakira, who took a message and insisted her daughter needed to attend a police station, before they could remove her from the missing list. Leila responded and arrived asking for Julian as instructed, who whisked her into an interview room.

"I can't stop now, but I am glad you are safe. This situation turned out to be serious!" he said gravely. "Jack and his mates have been admitted to hospital in Merseyside, apparently victims of an assault. This officer will need to take a statement from you as part of our new enquiry."

"Serves him right" she exploded impulsively as Julian was leaving the room.

Micky caught up with Shakira, demanding to know. "How well does Rocky know Jack, Shakira?"

"He doesn't, he's never met Jack!" she responded confidently as she had already given him the third degree "and he's only met Leila twice. I've never met Jack either, or Ethan for that matter" She went on,

"Leila did say Ethan knows Jack well, and is sure he was responsible for his robbery."

"Oh I see!" said Micky as if it had been reported. Then also rushing off, he yelled in her direction.

"Tell Julian I'm now going to see Jack Oop Norf"

Micky might have thought Jack Ahern was an ulcer on any policeman's bottom, but actually his concerned was for his welfare. Arriving at Arrow Park Hospital, the nurse apologised and told him they had all been discharged that morning. Jack had at least contacted Probation who had ordered him to stay at his Mum's, but the frail pensioner confessed they'd "Only just popped out to the pub." When Micky got to The Dale Inn a customer explained,

"Jack's Mum rang him here to say the bizzies had been round. Yesterday I saw them talking to some blert driving a VW transporter right outside the alehouse before they got beat-up and taken to the 'ozzy. They were back earlier today but disappeared again. Another hooligan turned up in an old Transit, it sounded like he was looking for Jack, but I don't know if he spoke to anyone but me."

While Micky was away, Ethan had been in a bit of a panic about the whole situation and in the end he rang Rocky who told Shakira,

"Ethan's conference at the Old Forge's with Nikos gave him the impression he was more interested in what her recent conflabs with the law might have evinced, rather than her welfare. Without admitting he had seen her, he convinced Ethan that he was keeping her out of it. He also promised him that because them 'micky mousers' had already been 'given the bum's rush' he would leave it at that with no more reprisals,"

Relating Ethan's story Rocky added, trying not to laugh,

"Apparently they stripped the dickheads of everything they had, including their jeans."

The next day, Shakira and Micky were trying to trace the second van, the first one clearly belonged to one of Nikos's clods. Shakira explained,

"The Transit had previously belonged to Nikos, but it had been sold on last year. It was registered to some bloke who gave a false name, and an address in the Midlands. When Diane went there and spoke to the occupants they'd had genuinely never heard of him".

"Thas a fierce ol bit of constabulary Shakira, but we've got a way to go yet" he praised.

She and Micky were still giggling about four idiots arriving at some A & E near the Wirral only in their shreddies, when he got an urgent message to meet Julian at the Norfolk and Norwich. He took her with him. When they got there Julian was talking quietly to a doctor. When he brought them up to speed they could tell he was dismayed and baffled to discover that Jack's friend Pascal had been pronounced dead at lunchtime. It was recorded as 'Accidental Alcohol Poisoning'.

Micky went off to admonish Leila at Bethel Street for the problems she had created by her absence, tearfully she told him

"I just went away to think for a while. Jack can stick any apology where the sun don't shine."

Micky said, "Who beat them up Leila?"

She was visibly taken aback, then as if she didn't believe his assertion responding aggressively with,

"How the hell should I know?" Actually Micky was pretty convinced she didn't know, so he said,

"Did you see Pascal?"

"I haven't seen any of them. Why what's *he* done?" She asked.

"OK, you can go Leila, but stay at your Mum's no more wandering off and causing havoc until we've sorted this out!" He said

Surprised and relieved no one mentioned Nikos whose input into the mix she felt responsible for, she left quick-smart.

Julian was insistent on Nikos accepting an invitation to accompany him at the nick, and when he and Diane questioned him, he started off by drivelling,

"Me bro' Ethan will tell you. I am safe now, a proper business man. Jack would tell you I been good, mi not tricky no more!" So Julian asked him,

"Why would you think Jack Ahern would have occasion to mention you Nikos?"

His response was calculated,

"Well I hear through them bush telegraph a bunch of amateur tek a beating up North, but me no have notin' to do with it, you can't think that." Nikos replied nonchalantly.

"Actually we can" Julian said "you and your mate picked them up in a VW transporter. What about the big fella Nikos, were you there when he was drinking a stupid load of vodka?"

"Vodka?" He spluttered "you make it up as you go along, that fat boy Pascal, friend of Derek son, de bafun, he chase me white rum last time we was limein'! De man no drink vodka"

"Alright you can go!" said Julian. "Oh one more thing, do you know who that is?"

Julian showed him a sketch. He said he didn't, but Julian caught a glimmer of recognition sweep over his eyes in the first split second.

After he left, Julian explained the picture to a confused Micky,

"This is a Flashface of the Transit driver seen outside The Oakland pub. It isn't Nikos or any of his nutters. Later a witness had seen Pascal being booted out of a Transit outside The Old Forge. As he phoned an ambulance someone else gave him CPR, before the other three came out of the pub. A local woman had seen Pascal speaking to the driver outside a pub in Merseyside. The boys said they had lost him in Wallasey and found him lying on the road back in Norwich 'with a crowd round him' as they say in Scouseland. He was dead before he got to hospital.

Micky said, "Bless me boy! Not only was this was no accident, but it was not Nikos either. The chap in Merseyside said the driver was northern but not scouse and certainly not cockney. Also Nikos knew Pascal's drink of choice was white rum, he knew he never touched vodka, yet he came back full of the stuff. It was Jack who liked vodka. Whoever picked him up in Wallasey then forced the vodka down him and dumped him in Norwich. Also when the first two found him he was still just conscious, as far as they could make out he said "I never upset Rocky's friend Ethan, I don't even know who the f*** Rocky is."

The both yelled, "He thought Pascal was Jack!"

Micky said "So we've got some psycho friend of Rocky's who also knows Ethan but not the difference between Pascal and Jack!"

Julian just said, "A psycho guilty of manslaughter or even murder!"

Chapter 4 Pop goes the Weasel

In an attempt to curb her natural instinct to abscond, Shakira and her new, well vetted computer, had been confined to a back room to explore another doubtful incident.

The apparent suicide of 1960's pop star Sid Hawkins had been featured in all the tabloids. She perused the cuttings and copious paperwork contained in the file, trying to get a sense of his character, or a clue to his possible propensity for self-destruction.

One news story included a background image of a beautiful thatched farmhouse in darkest Attleborough where, ostensibly where he met his end. She pondered over the photo in the hope staring at it might give her a window into the dreadful but undisclosed ordeal that had brought this successful man to his knees. An unknown secret whose repercussions might be so heinous, that it could lead a man of such copious talent, to a state of mind desperate enough, that in the comfort of his idyllic retreat he would end it all.

Theoretically, he had swathed his neck with a piece of brightly coloured rope which had been secured to a wooden beam, kicking the chair from under his feet to effect his demise. There was no note. The quantity of drugs and alcohol in his system was easily enough to distort his perspective, but not sufficient to render him unconscious. There had been no signs of him being dragged and he still sported bits of the ligature on his hands.

The reason an inquest was ordered had not been explained or recorded. Anna, his girlfriend had attended. Her testimony highlighted his constant inner struggles. An expert witness had concurred, verifying Sid's history of anxiety and depression. Even so, no one had predicted this extreme reaction, not even his long term soulmate.

As a suspect Anna lacked fiscal incentive. Before his departure, she already had possession of half the property and all and sundry had already pawed over her finances with a fine tooth comb. Shakira was confident their efforts left no possibility of any undiscovered, clandestine wealth. Psychologically Anna had been deemed an unlikely candidate anyway. It was felt, in her case, money would have been a weak and far-fetched motive to bump off her old man.

The only moot point, requiring further analysis, was the state of the room when Anna had apparently stumbled upon this grisly tableau. Aside from the obvious focus, the team noticed the immediate area around his corpse looked as it had been been ransacked. Shakira thought the team's first observations pretty conclusive and succinct. All except the appearance of some distinct but as yet undefined DNA.

Shakira followed the process in the notes from her lectures. Any probe into a death, must inherently include the possibility of murder. She felt the textbook 'who, what for and why' had already been exhausted. She was curious as to why she had been asked to chew over this tragedy and what serious evidence would warrant further invasion into these lives.

Gaining access to the crime site, while her seniors were embroiled in a potential 'Triad' murder at a newly discovered cannabis farm, was likely to be complicated. Her initial gambit was to sneak past the apparently empty outer office to a nearby pub.

The Francis Drake was picture postcard material. A lovingly preserved and recently re-thatched fourteenth century Coaching Inn. The picturesque garden was surrounded by a higgledy-piggledy series of small outbuildings. This was reputedly the birthplace of Sid's band, The Barbarians. A touch early for drinkers, the pub was empty apart from the guvnor, Austin, desperately trying to look busy in the tiny bar area.

To her delight, her initial probing questions about Sid, caused him to mistake her for a reporter, and his love of publicity was legendary which made extracting vital information a piece of cake.

"Oh yes!" he crowed "My friend Douglas, Sidney's roadie, loves the place and always likes to come here for lunch"

Helpfully he suggested that her best option would have been to sit patiently in a corner and wait for him to appear. As promised when he entered, Austin pointed with his eyes in her direction and asked him,

"Are you up to talking about Sid?"

"I suppose so" he sighed, picking up on his inference that she was from the press "as long as everyone leaves Anna in peace."

Shakira looked up inquisitively. Doug assumed that Austin, being the font of all gossip, would have already subjected any possible hack to stark interrogation and gently reproached her with,

"I'd have thought you lot would be sick of this story by now"

After employing copious amounts of diplomacy in her initial polite exchanges without giving away her real motive, she bravely asked him,

"Sid must have earned a few bob, might there be a secret stash of money somewhere?"

She thought his answer was pretty forthcoming,

"Not at all, off the record, he was pretty near bankrupt and his Mum's recent death had triggered a bout of depression which made it worse"

Then he quipped, "anyway the old bugger had an aversion to banks so if there was any cash, it would have been under the floorboards, and the rozzers had a good old nosey round everywhere, so I would assume he was indeed broke -unless you're inferring someone might have been there first!"

It occurred to her he was almost implicating Anna. It seemed an odd remark for someone who purported to be so protective, unless he had someone else in mind. Shakira touched upon the state of the studio. Doug pointed out placidly,

"Oh it usually looked as if he'd been burgled, and when he was on a bender he frequently went into over-drive, spraying papers around like confetti until he uncovered the object of his quest."

Shakira was curious about the term bender. She could not remember reading any hint that Sid might conform to the usual celebrity hell-raising, or financial squandering persona.

It occurred to her that she had gleaned very little from Doug's apparent forthright responses. On reflection, she concluded that while she was new to the game of extracting information, he was by now an old hand at dealing with questions and was pretty guarded in his answers.

Really she had wanted to start her enquiry with Anna, but was not sure how to approach this, or what the protocol was for a not quite fully-qualified policeperson to take this step. So despite still being theoretically confined to barracks, she crept out stealthily the next day, to prise a little more out of Austin.

Whatever vague ideas the man had about Shakira's profession, it was plain that Austin was fully aware that his first customer was a copper.

Micky, had already started eating lunch by the newly lit fire, whilst throwing the occasional piece of banter in Austin's direction at the bar. Unable to retreat unnoticed, Shakira stood nonchalantly as if he was invisible. He greeted her with,

"Oh there you are!" but before she responded, Micky put her out of her misery,

"We were waiting for you to turn up today, Julian had expected you would find it difficult to contain yourself, being so close to the premises, so when he saw you slip out again he rang me"

"It's a fair cop, guv", she relented waiting for another ear bashing, but he added,

"He was expecting me to conspire with you anyway, now as we have finished with the so called cannabis farm. I've arranged for Doug to come in with some of the band, they'll be here soon so ink your pen and smooth your notebook"

Still digesting his meal on the way out, he opened the door to leave, almost colliding with Doug as he entered. Pointing back at her with a jerk of his head, he announced,

"I'll leave you with my intern who is writing a thesis on previous investigations and won't need me mowing in, I'd better go back and show willing!"

Resigning herself to this sudden exposure and recognising Anna from the paper, she nervously waited for them to settle down by the now glowing hearth. When they looked comfortable she consulted her clip-board formally but awkwardly as if to begin, but Anna, rescuing her from recrimination, took charge,

"We were all going to the pub but Sid and I had a row" she began matter-of-factly.

Throughout this meeting Shakira thought she talked about Sid's death with a demeanour that exuded a business-like and almost aloof disposition. Although a year or so had passed, Shakira had expected a grieving widow, but surmised she may just play a better game of poker than the others. Anna continued her narration,

"He was in one of his moods, so I left him with his whisky and Doug and I took a taxi to The Crown. Doug dropped me off, somewhat worse for wear, before twelve".

Shakira realised, although this gave them both an alibi, somewhere in the back of her mind she was sure something was wrong with the timeline. She checked the notes discreetly. Yes, this *was* after his approximate time of death, but no phone call was recorded until the next morning. Where was Anna all night, and what wasn't she telling? Perhaps there was more to her relationship with Doug. She did not want to pursue this just yet, instead she listened intently while they each recalled the events. All of their versions included expressions of dislike and mistrust of one Hal Daly.

Further description of his character was unnecessary for Shakira. She was only too familiar with this particular piece of excrement you can't shift off your shoe.

This was because he had once almost caused Rocky to implement the usage of fisticuffs in a pub called The Sharks Tooth by attempting to fit-up his mate Pete with rape. Hal's motive for this asinine folly was apparently some sort of retribution. It had not turned out to be one of his better plans. Hal had told the police he had seen Pete leave the house of the victim moments after the crime. Not being the sharpest tool in the box, Hal had not checked some of the important details. Apart from the fact that Pete had a cast iron alibi, Pete was white and the rapist happened to have been black. An important factor when pointing the finger at a potential suspect, especially given the scarcity of people who could be categorised as BAME in Norfolk. To compound Hal's clumsy vitriol, not to mention his libellous assertions, the real perpetrator had already been identified, tried and banged up.

As a result of this nasty piece of shenanigans an angry Pete had brought his big mate Rocky to the pub and pointed out Hal to his uncompromisingly protective and loyal friend. Rocky's plethora of choice words in Hal's 'shell like', had the desired outcome, scaring the living daylights out of him and sending him packing, pronto. Hal was disappointed at being rumbled, especially by Rocky who he had hoped to be a potential coadjutor and who now recognised his maliciousness had exposed him as unequivocally intellectually challenged.

The recollection of this incident had led Shakira to conclude that faking a suicide would be way beyond his acumen, otherwise he would have been her prime suspect.

She felt she still needed to catch Anna alone, if only in order to discover what she was holding back and if it was pertinent to the situation. After gleaning her address from some notes, she threw caution to the wind and went to see her.

As she nervously approached the imposing chocolate box smallholding from the top of the driveway, she heard a couple of dogs barking in the main house. As had they not emerged to vet her, she was under the misapprehension that no one was home. No one answered her knock at the big front door, either. Still considering sensibly aborting her mission, she made one last ditch attempt. After exploring the surrounding outbuildings to seek another possible entrance and just as she took a path to the back of the house, Anna greeted her while emerging from a vegetable patch. Shakira was committed.

To her relief Anna beckoned her down yet another path that lead through a small herb garden. At the edge of a small orchard and in front of a converted barn was a table and four chairs and a lit chimera with an old fashioned coffee pot warming on it. Ignoring the dogs growling she chatted as she poured them both coffee.

"He called this his 'inspirational' workshop" She explained indicating the room just behind them, "he loved this old barn and the tiny recording kiosk at the back was where he wrote his songs. It was his little piece of paradise".

The previously private and almost abrupt woman who had appeared so blasé about her lover's demise, was now not only congenial but also emotionally vulnerable,

"It's self-contained then, Anna?" said Shakira pretending to sound business-like.

"Yes" said Anna "there is no access from the house or the other barns, and just at the moment I have no desire to go back in there."

Shakira was wondering why this had not been clarified in the report, and she could not help noticing the tear that began rolling down Anna's cheek as she spoke.

Ever cynical, it crossed Shakira's mind for a moment that this display might be for her benefit, but it was only a fleeting thought and soon scotched after a second glimpse of her weary expression. In fact she begun to feel a tad guilty. She realised Anna had been a dab hand at hiding her inner turmoil and her hunch about the poker face had been spot on.

Unperturbed by Shakira's scribbling, Anna now expressed herself softly, then deeper into the conversation in the sort of staccato created by quiet sobbing,

"It was the most dreadful thing that has ever happened to me. I had never even seen anyone dead before. At first glance I thought it was just one of his daft pranks until I tried lifting him up, he felt so cold and then it sunk in. I realised he had gone and that there was nothing I could do for him now. By the time the police came I was in bits. Maybe, just maybe, I could have stopped him!"

She composed herself for a minute and then continued tearfully,

"You see when he threw a tantrum I just left him to it, now I will never forgive myself, I just left him in the studio with his whisky. When the taxi dropped me home, I went straight to bed, I thought he would be sleeping it off." she began weeping gently again, "To see someone you love just hanging there with no life left in them and that awful colour. I will never get it out of my head. That vision will never leave me!"

Although the notes clearly stated she had been the 999 caller, Shakira had not considered before the impact that dreadful discovery would have had on Anna's emotional state.

Misinterpreting her pensive expression Anna realised that she had let the cat out of the bag and came clean.

"Well yes I should have made it clearer when they asked, but I didn't actually find him until the morning. The poor bastard strung up there like a meat carcass all night!" She sobbed before breaking down into uncontrollable tears. Shakira embraced her like a kindly aunt.

When she calmed down she muttered, "I realise I should have put them straight, but the press were already blaming me for his misery. Whatever he said publicly, he would often drink himself into oblivion, sleep it off and then be better in the morning!"

"What would have made him do it Anna?" Shakira asked gently,

"I don't know!" she sobbed "He'd been so weird lately. Although we'd had money problems and instead of *me* handling Sid's PR, horrible Hal was trying to muscle in. That's what the row was about. He had some hold over Sid's record company as well. I tried to persuade Sid to drop him, but although he reeked disaster Sid seemed almost powerless to distance himself."

Daft as he was, Shakira still had Hal down as a possible accomplice, should it turn out Sid's death had required some outside assistance.

Then Anna suddenly disturbed her own train of thought by, looking Shakira in the eye and yelling, "That's it! That's where I'd seen your face. You were there with your husband at The Sharks Tooth, when he tore Hal off a strip."

Shakira was at first a little alarmed by her revelation, but glad she had changed the subject.

"Your husband was the one person who had the balls to stand up to the nasty bully". She remarked warmly.

The likelihood that they had met before had not occurred to Shakira. Nor had she explored the possibility that Sid had also been present.

After this lucid conversation Anna seemed to have lost the plot completely when she blurted out aggressively,

"And who the hell was that manic bloke who turned up the next day. He told the police Hal was heading for a fall if he upset your husband again!" she giggled. This completely phased Shakira. Everything had made sense up until then now, but this comment was almost mitigating in Hal's defence.

"What manic bloke?" she blurted angrily

Anna just shrugged. "Never seen him before or since"

Suddenly the dogs who were still locked in the main house, changed from a series of growls, and started barking more loudly as if someone was breaking in. After checking there was no one about, Anna let them out. To Shakira's relief, the two Dobermans ignored her and went tearing down the driveway as if chasing someone, but after a short while came back slowly as if they had hit an invisible wall.

"A rabbit went past I expect" said Anna fussing them "Bloody useless pair, you could at least have caught me some dinner"

On her way back into work, Shakira bumped into Micky. Given the acquisition of this new information she felt duty bound to confess her extra-curricular chat.

As expected, she was reprimanded and reminded that her aberrant interrogation was out of bounds and worse than that, could not be used in court, should it prove necessary. Micky added,

"This loose cannon behaviour stops here Shakira, I've given you plenty of leeway and if Julian gets wind of this he'll go bananas. Aside from anything else, any re-examination of an inquiry should never have been disclosed to a possible suspect"

Micky put his chief wrist-slapper guise aside and went back to being coach.

"Then again. I suppose that was a fierce ol' bit of 'quality constaboolary' nevertheless Shakira"

He consulted her about how they could move on and perhaps undergo some damage limitation with Anna. As she had obviously built up a rapport with Shakira and had a well thought out 'best approach' he made an appointment for both of them to return the next week.

When Anna opened the door, Micky excused their presence pragmatically,

"Much as we don't like to intrude," he began diplomatically,

"We need to ensure that the circumstances surrounding your partner's loss are recorded accurately in the file. We need to clarify some of the chronology and correct any discrepancies we have in our original report."

However much Micky's objective was to nip this awkward situation in the bud, he knew the sudden renewed interest in past events would make Anna suspicious. Despite the visible ebb and flow of pain, she attempted to make some useful observations,

After re-iterating the series of events that led up to her horrific ordeal she said,

"On reflection his last bout of depression started straight after Hal and his numbskulls left here. Sid usually met them at The Francis Drake, so I was surprised when they had all emerged from the studio"

She sobbed a little and then said angrily.

"This is not for someone's college course! You're here because you think some bastard did this to him, don't you? You think one of them came back while we were in the pub!"

Micky did not answer. Then she said more pensively,

"You know Hal was keen on being Sid's PR man. I know Hal is not the sharpest knife in the box but he knew stringing Sid up would hardly get him a contract, even though I suppose Hal's predisposition to violent behaviour made tolerating his nonsense an easier option for Sid."

"This is a difficult question - but could he have known something about Sid he wanted to keep back, even from you?" Shakira asked watching for Micky's reaction."

"Well I did wonder if there was more to it." She answered with a strained verity.

When they returned to the office Micky went online to amend the file and as quietly as possible he read back his amendments and then said,

"I agree this should have been cleared up way before you found out, and that we have some useful information, but try and watch your step in future. No more doing your own thing please"

As if this remark prompted him he suddenly announced,

"Ah yes and Becky wants to see you"

"There is something about this whole thing we are not getting" Shakira added barely listening.

At the lab, instead of the expected rundown on forensics, Becky started what appeared to be a cross examination,

"I need to ask you about your movements before I look at some new evidence." Becky showed Shakira a Filofax in a plastic bag, and fired these words at her accusingly,

"Did you leave this at Anna's house the other day?"

"Absolutely not. I haven't seen one of those since the early eighties and I've never owned one!" Shakira replied, startled and bemused by the nature of the question.

Becky's marched out of the room throwing a sceptical "If you say so," over her shoulder.

Shakira tried not to show her concern and got chatting to a Lab Assistant.

"Can you tell me what's going on, Chris?" she asked pointing to the Filofax

"I don't see why not, Anna found it in the studio after you left her house. She doesn't think it's yours and we know it belongs to a Hal Daly".

"Oh?" she said, the penny dropping "We didn't even go in the studio, and what would I be doing with something belonging to that idiot?"

She did not continue as Chris had also been a little taken aback by Becky's tone and as if excusing her terseness he asked,

"If you are not busy at the moment would you like me to show you around?"

Shakira did not reply immediately because she was trying to fathom how Hal's Filofax could have so abruptly materialised there.

After about an hour of science Shakira was trying not to show her weariness, but did not want to upset her newly acquired ally. When Micky came in she expected to be rescued. Instead Shakira tried to ignore his eerie silence while he waited for Becky to return.

When Becky returned Micky handed her a small sealed bag and spoke to her quietly, but Shakira picked up snippets of their conversation even while she followed her new comrade,

"I meant to submit this earlier when Anna brought it in with the other item", he whispered "It's a key to the studio. It was still under the flower pot where Sid left it."

Then Becky pulled him out of Shakira's earshot and turned away behaving as if it was likely Shakira was the subject of their conspiratorial conflab. Irritated by this further insult, she thanked Chris loudly, and flounced away to her desk to ponder some of the subject matter of her evesdropping data.

Now, Becky was an uncomfortably efficient and tidy worker, almost to the point of OCD. So Shakira had been surprised that one of her just about audible assertions had been the miss-placement of some evidence.

When Micky returned, he made apologetic noises as if excusing the clandestine conference, adding

"I'm sorry I had to address the situation in the lab, oh yes and while I think of it Becky will require a sample of DNA from you and your husband for our records?"

As he made this sound like a normal procedure, she saw no reason not to comply and later persuaded a slightly reluctant Rocky to pop in to Bethel Street the next day. In fact none of this had phased her until she was looking up Hal's known associates. One name on the list was shouting at her. Rocky Browning!

Keeping this discovery to herself for the present, she was relieved to have previously mentioned to Micky Rocky's spat with Hal. She took this opportunity to 'follow up a lead' by requesting a chat with Sergeant Angel. Impudently she liked to call him by his favourite alias, Arc, as in Archangel. He had attended The Shark's Tooth after they had left.

"Confidentially, I didn't actually speak to the man myself", Sgt Arc recalled. "But a witness to the incident had apparently leapt to Rocky's defence. I was having a quiet word with Hal at the time, who we all had cited as the aggressor"

He was fond of Shakira who confided in him, "Actually Sarg" she started more persuasively "I'm more bothered by Rocky being listed as his 'known associate' partly because he can't stand the bloke. But mainly the only criminal record Rocky's ever had, was that one by Abba." she giggled,

Then she blustered, "Sorry who was this witness?" Trying not to shoot the messenger.

"While Hal had been desperate to convince me that he and Rocky were bezzie mates, apparently this other chap vehemently took exception to his assertion. He wouldn't give her a name but wait a minute," He read Diane's description from his pocket book "Northern accent, of average height, greasy dark longish hair over his face, grey sideburns, scruffy but short beard and a rash. You'll need to talk to Micky and find out who put Hal on ECINS."

Micky was not fazed by Rocky's name on the computer. He seems much more concerned about some issue with Becky.

"How long were you in the lab before I got there, Shakira? You didn't touch anything did you?" he asked,

"What an odd question, of course not, I'm not an idiot" She responded tersely.

After a while he resumed confiding in her,

"We have discovered Sid received online threats that Anna was not aware of and we don't know who made them or why, but it was definitely not Hal. Anna said we need to talk to their old bassist, Eric who works at the tin factory."

Shakira pointed out "Rocky worked there briefly, I'll see if he knows him".

"OK, but tread carefully Shakira, I don't want to get wrong with Julian again."

When Shakira asked Rocky, he could only vaguely remembered Eric as he had worked in another plant. He couldn't place the other fella in the pub either,

"Sounds like Kenny McCann" he giggled.

"I think we would noticed if *he* turned up at the tin factory, anyway he's in America." Shakira scoffed "It could be any of the scruffy herberts round here who want to be your bezzie mate".

Armed with the little information Rocky had given Shakira, Micky went into the works canteen to pose as a new agency worker and was just chatting to Eric's pal when a chap he had once arrested walked in to the canteen. He made himself scarce, pronto deciding to contact their agency instead. The consultant explained Eric was no longer on her books. She sighed,

"Quite frankly we were glad when the company took him on directly, he moaned a lot and kept harping on about unions and worker's rights, drove me nuts"

To his relief she gave Micky Eric's address. His heart hadn't in been his attempt at undercover work this morning and the noisy, greasy factory was hardly conducive to a professional interview. When Micky turned up at Eric's house, he was busy fussing around his Mum. She clearly had dementia and kept asking Micky if he'd come from the hospital.

"I never made any threats to anyone, let alone Sid, he'd have chinned me" Eric responded only half listening.

"I *know* that, but these were done from an untraceable computer" Micky retorted "but we're had trouble finding its location." Micky realised this technophobe was a very unlikely suspect, but as he was happy to give his DNA and fingerprints in the hope of getting rid of the police it was not a wasted visit. Micky explained they always carried kits and Shakira watched him seal it in the bag carefully.

"By the way", Micky added, "was the scruffy bloke hanging round the Shark's Tooth a friend of yours?" Eric looked at him as if he'd just spoken from Mars.

Later Micky rang Hal and requested he came in to collect his property. Shakira heard him at the desk protesting petulantly,

"It was very inconvenient. It was sure it must have been nicked in the pub, I've got a crime number. Now you are saying it turned up in Sid's studio. Whoever stole it from me must have planted it there."

Shakira overheard this from behind the front desk where she was standing with Micky. She took umbrage particularly at the word 'planted' which was noticeably thrown in their direction.

She looked at Micky and shouted at him theatrically, loudly enough for the entire station to hear.

"Well it certainly wasn't me, *I've* never been in the bloody studio!" This confounded Hal a little and blatantly somewhat baffled Micky. He didn't realise she had never actually been in Sid's room either.

Away from the counter Shakira remarked, "Well, I suppose he did report it missing and it's definitely his"

"You seem surprised, had you assumed he lied about the theft, Shakira?" Asked Julian,

"Well actually no, and that surprised me. It was quite a shock to hear even a modicum of anything from his gob that resembled the truth" She quipped "Refreshing as honesty may be in his case, it bothers the hell out of me."

"What are you getting at, do you think it *was* planted?" spluttered Julian

"Well the whole thing strikes me as a bit too Agatha Christie" she remarked skating on thin ice.

"Its sudden appearance seemed as strange to me as it supposedly did to Hal, but before I get hauled over the coals again, I'm not suggesting it was one of your precious policeman!" she replies sarcastically and bordering on insubordination.

"*Someone* else has been playing silly buggers if you ask me. Horrible as Hal is, if he and his cronies pooled their brain power, I doubt they'd be able to wipe their own botties, all on their own without help. I can't see them planting evidence, let alone staging a hanging!"

Arthur had been listening carefully. Whatever reservations he had about her tone, he was prompted to interject.

"If indeed if we are looking for some surreptitious intrigue, I have to agree he makes a poor subject. We must get this business sorted, before one of our overseers takes it off our hands".

Recognising his thinly veiled threat had hit home, Arthur started to leave. Thinking he was already out of earshot, Julian brought something on his phone to Micky's attention.

"One of Eric's band mates blamed 'Rocky's Missus' for accusing Eric of exacerbating Sid's suicide" he complained, "Look at Shakira's reply on Eric's timeline",

"Bit close to home again Shakira" Arthur chipped in.

"It's can't be me can it" she remonstrated "I can't access Facebook on this thing and they've still got my iphone!"

"Blimming hell!" Micky yelled, then he muttered as he left the room.

"I'm going to have this hacker for breakfast, he do give me some misery!"

"You seem to have a lot of security issues Shakira" Arthur chimed in accusingly, not having paid attention,

"Yes!" said Julian, "the computer then the missing DNA!"

"What DNA?" she asked him.

Before he had a chance to answer Micky returned waving a piece of paper.

Realising he had said too much Julian slipped away pronto "Why is he going on at me about DNA?" she asked Micky angrily.

"I don't know, what is he like?" he said awkwardly, "Come on Shakira let's see if we can catch this bozo at it in the library"

No one had ever seen Eric in the library at any time, for any reason.When they got to his home it sported a conspicuous lack of techno-gadgets about the place.

"I said no such thing" Eric had remonstrated on the phone "I barely know the bloke and I haven't got a bloody smartphone anyway. No disrespect but it's been common knowledge that Rocky's missus used to know the band, before she worked with you. Someone's pulling your plonker!"

Despite his irritation, he gave Micky a list of 'musos' phone numbers who might know who this joker was. Micky read out an email from Becky.

"Apologies to Shakira. The mysterious DNA has been recovered after a phone call to last year's temp lab assistant. I had assumed it was lost. She had wrongly listed it as having been identified, instead of 'dormant, no match found' where the blessed thing should have been"

This was the nearest to swearing Shakira had heard from Becky, she would have laughed if she had not been so incensed by her attitude in the first place.

"What a surprise!" Shakira remarked aggressively "the 'blessed thing' was not a match to Rocky after all, not even a match to me! I'm surprised poor old Eric wasn't in the frame"

 "Well that's that then!" said Julian. "The CPS have decided to put this case to bed. They cited lack of evidence to indicate that Sid's death was anything but by his own hand".

"Hang on a minute. What about the first missing and still unidentified DNA and the floating Filofax?"

Shakira protest, directed at Julian, was met with his awkward silence.

Chapter 5 Fast Eddie

There is no question that Eddie Alba had been a naughty boy in his time, but now he was virtually retired. He had relinquished his involvement in his past businesses, legal and otherwise to lead a comparatively quiet life as a dodgy landlord.

Of course this charismatic rogue still felt it was his duty to indulge in the hectic banter bouncing recklessly off the walls of the nearby licensed premises. He could not have his competitors in the latest bout of wicked and scathing cockney humour, thinking they had the edge. Eddie was a shrewd, intelligent, independent thinker, who was generous to a fault. His sensitive nature was scarcely concealed under his wide boy exterior. He inhabited a tiny flat in the heart of London that suited his purposes.

On a rare trip back to the wicked city, Shakira and Rocky decided to visit Eddie's chaotic and highly suspect local pub, hoping to discover him lurking about the place and up to no good. Most of their old London mates had either moved away or were working early doors, so catching up with Eddie was a real bonus. They arrived just as the guv'nor unlocked the battered entrance, and just as the first of the scruffy local junkies wandered in plying their trade in stolen goods. Conveniently, all merchandise was the same price as a bag of smack.

Eddie sat reading the sports page, dressed in expensive designer clothes and prominent gaudy bling with the obligatory Pringle jumper which had never seen the light of a golf course. Shakira and Eddie had remained friends long after she worked for him, and he treated Rocky like visiting royalty. After he and Rocky consumed several libations, he offered them a big couch in his small flat. After a call to the child minder, Shakira ditched the orange juice and ordered a proper drink. The caricatures contained within his anecdotes were so accurate, that if a subject of his recent mirth had the misfortune to waft in unsuspectingly off the street, they were greeted with a raft of stifled laughter.

While in the midst of a particularly animated narration, concerning the well-deserved misfortune of some daft, would be bad boy that had resulted in a holiday courtesy of Her Maj, he broke off suddenly.

Giving Shakira a serious look, he spoke in a soft voice, "Did you hear what happened to *your* old mate Byrnesy?"

"Oh gawd what's he done now?" asked Shakira who expected some criminal exploit to be forthcoming.

"Drowned in the bath" said Alby

Shakira was visibly shocked. She had always known Emanuel Byrne could be a right pain in the arse when he was drunk, was given to gratuitous violence, and was more than probably a wife beater. Despite this and the dreary insignificance of their long ago one night stand, she would not have wished anything as awful as death on the dopey sod.

"What happened? Did someone drown the bastard?"

"Well the old bill reckoned he slashed his wrists in the bath; he was full of drink and Prozac and the shock drowned him before he bled out, but I'm not so sure!"

Shakira was not so sure either. Manny seemed an unlikely suicide victim and she was not so sure under the circumstances of Alby's description. Her colleagues had often said the local branch of the Met were slapdash, but she had assumed this assertion had been part of the professional rivalry with the force from the next borough.

"I had to clear up the mess as he was living in one of my gaffs." He said trying to pretend the discovery had not horrified him. "His veins was not just cut across, but pierced with a knife by someone who knew exactly how to do it quick. Unless Byrnesy had acquired a secret medical degree I can't imagine it was him. The old bill said they often made sure they die speedily, presumably so as no one dragged him down the Whittington to be patched up!" He said gravely.

"What do you mean the mess, Alby?" she enquired naively.

"I had to scrub all his claret off the bathroom walls and the ceiling, even in the hallway and repaint the whole place!" He said "I've seen people dead before but…." he trailed off as Shakira interrupted.

"Topping yourself in the bath with the door opened, sounds unlikely to me!"
"Yeh actually I could see the bathroom door was opened when I got in. I didn't need to go any further to know he'd copped it, I could smell him as soon as I put the key in the front door" He mumbled still re-living the moment.
"I had to come out and ring the old bill from the street"
"Poor bugger" said Shakira sadly
"I wouldn't feel too sorry for him", Alby replied thoughtfully,
"He kept grilling me for your address when you left!"
"Whatever for, I haven't seen him for years?" She asked still not quite following his inference.
The answer began to dawn on her as Alby explained.
"According to the grapevine he had some scheme to get money out of the gang on your estate, he pretended he had your new address, but none of them was bothered. In the end they were fed up with the earache so one of the little scroats lumped him"
"I doubt any of them done him. Most of them are still indoors," Shakira replied.
"Nah, but he was trying to impress some hoodlums from South of the River that knew his pathetic sister. Well you know what he was like, he could barely go to the shop on his own without a minder"
"So do you think it was them who topped him Alby? His sister did mix with some dubious tossers, could have been one of her druggie mates."
"Well I dunno, he was in fine fettle that night, he was his usual badly behaved drunken self in that Italian place up the passage. As soon as he spotted Splosh and some of the waiters from his posh restaurant through the window, they knew he was going to invite hisself over. They only stopped about ten minutes after he muscled in, then they all buggered off before he got slung out. He was rabbiting on about the car he just bought, so if he was got at, it was much later." said Alby knowingly "The knob-heads that hung around with his horrible sister are favourite, they was nasty bastards them!" he recalled.
"You couldn't forget her and her smack habit.Is she still with the same scrawny twat who used to flog her the gear?" asked Shakira

"Oh yeah" he replied "more than a bit warm that lot, they all tapped Manny for a few bob. Perhaps he did do hisself in, after the bastards bankrupted him!" Eddie spluttered with more than a bit of venom.

Shakira took all this with a pinch of salt as she knew Eddie would have rescued him before any bailiffs came knocking. Just when her burning curiosity for an unsolved crime was getting the better of her, she saw Splosh across the pub and waved furiously. He was delighted to see the "pair of old tarts!" and greets her and Rocky warmly.

The word camp is not enough to describe Splosh, but perhaps outrageously flamboyant would be a start. In all Splosh's stories about the exploits of the local 'butch mafia,' he referred to the men as *she* or *that old queen,* regardless of their proclivities. He recounts the evening before Eddie found Manny.

"Oh there was nothing wrong with *her* that night!" he said "She was her usual pissed and obnoxious bloody self, upsetting all the waiters demanding some Italian cheese she couldn't pronounce. Then she was running on about her new motor and some win on the geegees!" We managed to slip out when the junkie sister turned up with some other bell-ends. I bet she got stuck with their tab, she always did. I don't know what miss bossy boots had over the daft old queen, but I bet they all took the living piss and it's not that cheap that *Acquelina's* you know, even if you only have a drink!"

Splosh thought Manny was a nuisance but only in the sense he was uncultured and not very bright which made him somewhat of a liability, rather than someone who deserved to be done in. Some old bloke they had dubbed 'Slippery' joined in with his 'two-penn'th',

"Byrnesy was in a pub in Hackney the week before with some "old sort" in tow. Her Yardie boyfriend turned up, fresh from Jamaica and built like a brick shithouse. Perhaps he took exception to her messing with the likes of Byrnesy, perhaps *he* offed him". He paused for breath and then garbled,

"He's a nasty bit of work 'en all, you ask Fast Eddie, he knows him!" He blurted out this impassioned warning before realising he had used Alby's rather more poignant nickname, not only in his company but within his earshot!

"Well, my 'friend' Joe wanted to kill Byrnesy over the homophobic jokes, I know she puts on her 'gay rights knickers' and gets them in a right old twist at that sort of thing, but she doesn't mean any harm." interjected Splosh.
As the pub filled up and the gossip was fuelled by booze there were lots of theories about how Byrnsey met his end, but the general consensus of opinion amongst the company was that someone had helped along Byrnesy's exsanguination.
Shakira was quite aware that Manny Byrne's had sported a talent for making enemies an awful lot quicker than he made money, and aiding and abetting his demise would have attracted plenty of candidates. She also knew he often invited people back to his hovel for a drink, without vetting them properly. Nevertheless, turning him over for a bit of dosh was a far cry from purposefully, not just slitting but piercing the poor bastard's wrists. It was too much of a stretch, and anyway what would he be doing having a bath at that time of night instead of his usual bottle of scotch?
The next morning three of them, still in yesterday's attire, ate a quick breakfast in the caff next door. Shakira put it to Alby that this quandary might be worth running past one of her colleagues.
"Well alright," said Alby "but keep my name out of it. The filth already know I found him, and I don't want to end up in the frame!" There was no love lost between Eddie Alba and the police.
Rocky voiced a thought that was visibly amusing a smirking Shakira,
"I don't think the police would come after you Alby" he started playfully "after all you're a good boy these days. Especially after that bent copper spoke up for you, when you got let you off for that bit of Charlie" he joked. Then he added,
"Shakira, couldn't you have a quiet word with that Micky bloke you work with? He seems to have a bit of nous, so he would be able to tell you what to do!"
Alby said "I can't see any of the contenders wanting to talk to the bill"
"Like who?" Shakira asked,

"Well his sister and her cronies are favourites. Then there was Splosh's boyfriend Joe, he couldn't stand him. And Paige's boyfriend Errol, who was seen lurking near the flats that night and some other random fella rang the intercom and got let in." Shakira laughed "At that time of night when they've just kicked out of 'Barnet' to gravitate towards Upper Street. Every North London nutter is loitering about the place, up to no good. Look, if someone did croak him, they should be brought to book"

However uncomfortable he felt taking the moral high-ground Alby had to agree.
When she returned to her desk in the broom cupboard cum office, Shakira had been left a pile of work and Micky was running round like a headless chicken. Although it was old news, she did not want Byrnsey's death to be ignored, so she made up a file with her evidence so far, and asked Micky to have a look at it when he had time.
The next day he came to tell her that the CPS had Sid's death down as a definite suicide. None of the new revelations had changed that verdict.
Shakira was not impressed,
"They seem to have washed their hands, quicker than I do in the public lav on the market" She changed the subject.
"What about Manny, the bloke I told you about in London. Did you get to read my essay?" she reminded him
"I might have done" he joshed
"It's not under our jurisdiction" he grinned purposely winding her up,
"Julian faxed it to some chap he knows in the Met. They wouldn't have taken kindly to some bumpkin Sergeant trying to interfere in a cold case. Why didn't these people come forward before?"
"Nobody talks to the police in London, Micky. They'd start petrol bombing your house." she quipped.
Micky stopped joshing her,
"Look Shakira, when I've cleared up some of this old squit, we'll arrange to meet up with your friend. I'll tell Julian it is part of a 'joined up justice' project, or something".

A week or so later, Shakira took Micky to meet Alby. He had told Shakira he would be the next one down the plughole if she brought a copper into his local. They met at the York Tavern in Soho, a place he thought was far away enough from his manor. Alby explained to Micky he had doubts about the likelihood of Manny topping himself, skilfully avoiding mentioning any names. So Micky gave him a little push,
"If someone did help him paint the bathroom red, who's your money on?"
Relenting he took a quick shufty round and mumbled,
"I don't really have a clue but I suppose it could have been Mad John, who was one of the sister's lackeys. Her boyfriend Todd is a nutcase 'en all. Then there is Paige's Errol, he can be a right slag and Splosh's Joe. He wouldn't have been short on volunteers. I haven't really got a Scooby who croaked him."
Shakira remembered Mad John. In fact, not many people bothered Shakira, but with this psychopathic pest it was worth keeping your distance. She recalled his ability to clear a pub single handed, hospitalising the entire clientele with his own fists.
"What the bleeding hell was Manny associating with him for?" she asked
"He sold his sister smack, amongst other things Shakira. She's mad for it!" he replied.
On the way back, she and Micky walked through the back alleys to Byrnsey's former home as Micky bleated.
"You know I'm only getting half the bloody story Shakira"
"If I found it difficult to talk to you about the surrounding den of iniquity, he must have been way out of his comfort zone!" she explained. They stopped for coffee so she could show him the proximity to the main drag, then returned to Wymondham.
Shakira considered the suspects. Errol was a formidable presence but dark skinned enough to be reasonably distinctive. Someone would have noticed him enter the building. She understood Joe's dislike of gay bashers, but his objection was more political than psychotic. The sister's boyfriend was doing time in The Ville up for selling class A's with Mad John.

Manny had hated all drugs even if there was money in it so he was unlikely to have trodden on their toes by moving in on their patch. Realistically she was stuck for anyone with a serious motive.

Meanwhile, after he had been given the go ahead by whoever Julian had badgered at Holloway nick, Micky's mate Bobby who had who been a "wooden-top" in nearby Upper Holloway for long enough to be dubbed 'The' Bobby walked into the caff. In uniform, and with no intention of subtlety, he 'happened' upon Errol and plonked himself down nearby. Instead of the usual "what now" attitude he expected of a serial scumbag, Errol was very polite and explained,

"I'm out on licence so I'm keeping good, boss"

"Tell me about Byrnsey!" Bobby demanded. So out of the corner of his mouth Errol mumbled,

"Look, Byrnesy and I were mates not rivals boss. Whether or not he slashed his own wrists I dunno, but I never done it boss. I was outside the pub having a fag when this scruffy looking bloke pressed the intercom and went into the flat, but I never seen him before or since"

Before too many punters started 'earolling' the conversation, he grinned and politely requested that Bobby should either arrest him or find another place to eat breakfast or at least, that was the gist.

Having genned up his Sarg that he had intel about a suspicious death, but without saying his source was another copper, Bobby went to point out some facts to Alby.

"It being obvious" he said "that subletting your 'daughters' place to Manny had been illegal and as her current accommodation was 'temporarily elsewhere,' I see no reason not to let me in without a warrant, do you?"

"As you put it so courteously I suppose you'd better come and have a butchers!" Alby replied.

Bobby did not remark on the possessions of the current residents strewn about the place, as Alby ran through the events preceding his friend's untimely end. Bobby was now even more convinced that none of the afore-mentioned, possible suspects were involved. He needed to find the unknown person, the one no one admitted answering the intercom to. He knew by now this abode would contain the finger-prints and the DNA of half North London's criminal fraternity.

However afterwards Alby was able to recollect something not documented before. He rang Shakira to say Manny had complained that someone had broken in about a week prior to his death, a fact which had genuinely slipped the mind of Eddie Alba. For the life of him the man they nicknamed Fast Eddie could not think of anyone who would have a key. Nor had he found, a conclusion to the enigma of this injustice that satisfied him. But he was still working on it. Bobby, Shakira and Micky were not far behind him in that respect.

Chapter 6 Bad Rubbish

Before she met Blake Darcy, Tamara Quayle had managed to survive her somewhat disorderly lifestyle without a man in tow for some time. That said, her life had been far from easy, even without a man complicating the issue.

Blake was either not aware of, or not interested in, her former 'business arrangements' Which ever it was she felt she had carte blanche to accept his gifts as generosity rather than payment. Previously she had split with a violent husband which had cut deep into her mental wellbeing, but Blake seemed different at first. True, there were some things in his nature that made her a little uncomfortable but she could not put her finger on exactly what. At first she dismissed her misgivings, turning a blind eye to the effects of his heavy drinking and boyish 'hard-man' boasts. There had been a couple of worrying spats, but nothing like previous wounds from men who couldn't keep their fists to themselves.

Blake was a popular bloke in Norwich pubs so his friends treated her with respect. 'Mara' as everyone called her, liked to think she was old fashioned girl, so she never asked Blake about his employment. She hoped this lack of curiosity about his livelihood would keep him from asking awkward questions about hers. In any case, she had always pretended to herself that her cash transactions had been agreements between friends and nothing to do with turning tricks.

Blake had a background in the building trade. He had met Mara whilst undertaking odd jobs for the caretaker in her flats. As indirectly his employment was Council funded, although probably off the cards, it was easy for her to convince herself, that all his income was legal. After all, none of his mates had implied anything else. In truth she suspected the source of his income was for the most part spurious, if not downright criminal.

Whatever ideas she had about his earnings, *he* was perfectly well aware of her past exploits. In fact he had always liked the company of working girls, who he regarded as easy to please, despite Mara's romantic notions. The trouble was they both liked booze and boozers. Recently, his drinking bouts had been clouding his judgement and alcohol had begun to conjure up some old demons whilst Mara's drinking was sending her back to a dark place.

As the tentativeness of the hold Blake had on his own sanity had become more prominent, he had begun to take his frustration out on Mara. Her drunkenness began to leave her without the wherewithal to defend herself. She told herself she must stop making excuses for him, and get the hell out. She knew extricating herself from Blake's little world would prove difficult. Their lives had become so intertwined. Eventually one evening, she actually felt relieved when he took himself home to sleep off an all-day session. She took herself back to one of her old haunts and picked up another man, Albert.

Albert had a legitimate and generous income and a more placid nature. It was easy for Mara to convince this lonely older man, that he was her knight in shining armour, rescuing this damsel in distress. Blake, did not know the locale of his little suburban enclave, so Mara was convinced she had found a safe haven for a while. Which indeed it was, until one day when she looked at her old phone.

In amongst the myriad of missed calls from Blake demanding her return, there was an unexpected text from her neighbour Ada. It said Mara had had had a break-in. When Mara rang her Ada spoke calmly and assured her nothing was missing and that as she had a set of keys, she was happy to deal with the repair man when he arrived the next morning to replace a small piece of glass. Mara insisted this was her responsibility and promised to turn up early to let him in. When the man knocked on Ada's door at lunchtime asking where Tamara was, Ada had a bad feeling. Fickle as she was with other people, Mara had never broken a promise to Ada. She unlocked the door for him and he confirmed no one was in. Almost as if he was spooked, he left without fixing the door on the pretext of an immediate appointment on his busy schedule, while Ada rang the police.

This was as far as the written profile of this potential crime victim took Shakira. Her journey into the life of this woman was curtailed at this juncture by a collective impression that she had evaporated into thin air. Nevertheless the missing person's report showed the case was far from atypical so Shakira could only assume its high profile must stem from the recent publicity surrounding the Suffolk Strangler. This not only accounted for Arthur's licence to intervene in an ostensibly still opened case, but was presumably his justification for the unnecessary shroud of secrecy he had wrapped around it.

Mara's Probation Officer had kept an almost intrusive diary until that morning. Although the coppers who eventually attended had ticked all the boxes, checking the obvious places etc. Shakira thought the previous investigation unimpressive. More recently Diane and Liz had been deployed on some door to door, but to no avail. They searched the local fields and outhouses and briefly sent up the helicopter but there was no trace.

With Julian's permission, Shakira had already quizzed Albert on the phone,

"Mara had insisted on going back to sort it out by herself despite my protests." He explained, "She had promised to ring if she had any problems. When she did not return, or answer my calls, it seemed possible that she was back with Blake. Of course I was a little worried, especially as he'd been violent with her. At the end of the day I did not want to interfere but naturally I was upset at the time. Even when I found out she had apparently disappeared, I still presumed she would turn up in one piece when she fancied."

She had perceived no discernible deceit in his narrative so she went to see Ada who regarded Mara's absence with much more circumspection.

"I bet that husband of hers had a hand in this. They had some order out to bring him back from Spain if they catch up with him, so you won't see hide nor hair of him"

"Actually that was dealt with a while back he's now on an oil rig" responded Shakira "We will be having a word when he's back onshore!"

"Blake did knock on the door once, but I told him she was with someone else" Ada recalled with glee "He just shrugged his shoulders and walked off looking uninterested, so I doubt it was him who broke the glass as he would have asked me to give her a message if he had been that bothered. What did Albert think, you know the bloke she was shacked up with?" Ada asked.
"He thought she'd gone back to Blake, he didn't know she'd been missed until recently" she blurted out, disclosing more than she meant to.
Shakira thought she better take her leave before she elucidated any further. She went to find Micky who was clearly in no panic to find Blake, even though Shakira was convinced that even if he was not a suspect, he had been deemed a catalyst to Mara's absence. According to staff at The Bull, he also appeared to have also melted into the ether, along with his bar tab.
"What about Blake? Shakira reminded Micky insistently,
"I would have been informed if he'd scarpered. He's still on probation and as he had shown genuine concern for Mara's welfare, I don't have any reason to accuse him of foul play just yet!" he assured her.
In contrast Alan's reaction to her absence seemed downright cavalier. To begin with he refused to open the door to Micky.
"I've just finished a night shift" he moaned "come back when I've had some kip," Micky took his attitude with a pinch of salt.
"He's an awkward bugger and a bit of a lone wolf. He used to work on the old Travelling Post Office, you know the night train, and didn't take to being back at the sorting office" said Micky "he's no angel but his penchant was for pub brawls, not domestic violence"
"Not that one precludes the other" she added swiftly.
Later Micky asked a more compliant and less fractious Alan,
"Did you break the glass in her door Alan?"
"I haven't seen her, what makes you think it wasn't Blake's fault, he's handy with his fists" he whined. Satisfied with his response at present, Micky left it at that. It was apparent Alan did not regard her departure as cause for alarm either.

As they left, Micky explained to Shakira "When two reprobates start grassing each other up, you can bet they are in cahoots over something." He had suspected the pair of them had been plotting some witless piece of skulduggery for some time, but regardless he planned to talk to Howard the caretaker first. Shakira regarded Howard's description of the person he had seen running away, albeit in the dark, as curiously vague. Apart from moaning about having to repair the glass in the door himself, he seemed fairly blasé about a missing tenant. Ada had blamed local vandals but Howard told Micky,
"No, it definitely wasn't a kid I saw, I suppose it could have been Blake, or Alan." He added "I'm not sure who it was, but Mara's done a bunk before when she's short on rent money, she'll turn up again!" Shakira wondered why Ada had not caught a glimpse of this character too. After all, she had come out when she heard the glass go and was adamant no one was around. Shakira's unrequited curiosity was frustrated by Micky's continued lack of interest in Blake, so she was pleased when, after a phone call he smiled and capitulated,
"Alright then Shakira, let's go to the Pumpkin, Blake is dossing in some flop-house round the corner with a bunch of no-goods!" He explained his sudden change of heart on the way,
"This morning, Ada had stopped Liz and Diane on the Estate. Apparently someone had been seen loitering at the back of Mara's flat. Then in the early hours of the morning she thought a noise disturbed her sleep. Ada gave Liz the keys and asked them if they would take a look just in case someone had got in. Although empty, as soon as they entered the flat there was an awful smell, only slightly masked by a strong smell of bleach. Barely visible were smudged marks on the floor where someone had tried to clean up a substance that resembled blood. When Diane poked her head round the door. Ada was still behind her, waiting on the walkway so she stood blocking the doorway, to cover the brutal scene and probably her own horror. She told Ada it was empty but Ada was somewhat bemused and suspicious when they requested to keep the keys, but she took the hint anyway and went back indoors. They locked the door behind them and rang Julian. He's on his way there now with SOCO. He wants me to pick up Blake."

As Micky had surmised Blake was languishing in The Pumpkin. Ostensibly he had been there all day drinking and his demeanour seemed to confirm his alibi. Micky and accompanying burly officers told Shakira to keep out of the way in case he was a handful. He wasn't and by the time they reached Wymondham he was almost coherent,
"Me and Mara had just grown apart" he mumbled, not fooling anyone "I wasn't even told she'd gone missing. I didn't even know she'd took up with the old bloke until recently!"
"What about her door?" Micky asked, "Did you break in?"
"Why would I?" he remonstrated.
"I could have got my keys back anytime. I'm living with a better looking woman now," he whined, still not fooling anyone.
The fact that he had been holed up in a squat round the corner made it clear his drinking had become paramount. Despite his lies and the likelihood that he was violent towards women, Shakira was not convinced this sad excuse for a man was responsible for Mara's disappearance. If he had done her any harm, she doubted he would have the wit to cover his tracks that well. Blake did not give any hint that he knew the flat had actually been entered, so Micky did not bring it up,

Anyway, Shakira now agreed that Alan was just as likely a suspect. If Blake was at all culpable then it was likely were in cahoots. She hoped this was not the case, as she understood a 'cut-throat defence' (blaming each other) was a solicitor's nightmare making it difficult to convict.
Later that week, local community coppers told Liz about an almighty punch-up in The Pumpkin, normally a reasonably quiet family pub. They mentioned it because it started with aggravation between two men, Alan and Blake. "They had been as thick as thieves in the Bull, just the night before" Diane added astutely.

The rabble in The Pumpkin did not know Liz, so she sipped wine quietly at a table in plain clothes. While the bar staff were discussing the fight, one of them nipped off to the Ladies. As it was quiet Liz followed and flashed her warrant card discreetly without fear of disturbance. As the woman explained they'd had to ban Blake and Alan because of the damage, Liz showed her a photo,
"Do you recognise this woman called Tamara or Mara?" she asked "or was she mentioned in the row?" The woman explained "No, she wasn't mentioned, but I have seen her with Blake before. Actually it was a funny conversation really, they did not talk about women at all. They were going on about Alan's dustbin and something Blake had done to it, perhaps he recycled the wrong plastic, I dunno."
When she told Micky, Julian quipped "Recycling *stolen* plastic more like. We need to haul these two over the coals and find out what kind of chicanery they were fighting over!"
When the lab results came in, they confirmed the blood was Mara's. Although it was strangely diluted, there was enough to indicate a possibly fatal injury. There were no signs of a break in but there were drag marks by the back door.
Shakira pointed out,
"The perpetrator must have entered by the front door to unlock the back and drag her out. Where the hell was she until now?"
"When she went missing, they checked the place thoroughly and it was spotless." Micky piped up, "that don't make no sense because they are sure it was not fresh!"
Meanwhile, a homeless man was seen looking for some leftovers round the back of the Kebab House that was just round the corner from both Blake and Alans. Suddenly he entered the shop yelling. It sounded like a drunken complaint about health and safety at first. Despite his incoherence, the chef had decided to follow him out and find out what the fuss was about. He had made a most macabre discovery. He thought someone had dumped some bad meat, until he moved the bag away from himself, because it smelt rank. Suddenly a hand fell out. He rushed back in and rang the police.

These shocking events went round the cop shop like wildfire. In fact they were so unusual in sleepy Norfolk that they hit the national papers. What they did not report was that some bits of the woman were missing. The next day two Regional Crime Squad detectives arrived to 'interfere'.
Still no one had connected the two gory discoveries until, Shakira woke up the whole station by screaming,
"Of course dustbins!"
"Do what John?" said Micky, taking the micky in his best cockney!
"My woman in The Pumpkin said Blake and Alan were arguing about bins!" she retorted in her best 'Naafuk' "they must have put Mara's body in bin-bags" she added as if it was crystal.
"Those two, cutting up a body, seems unlikely" Julian said thoughtfully, "but it's too much of a coincidence, let's have both the buggers back in Michael!"
Alan was in The Fisherman's Arms at a beano, with a load of postmen including Rocky when a policemen and a PCSO came in. The policeman requested politely that Alan came to the station for a chat. Rocky neither knew about the case, nor had he a clue that Shakira had a hand in its investigation, nor indeed that his colleague might have been involved in a serious crime. So when Alan asked Rocky's advice, he assumed this obtrusion from the pleasure of his next beer was for something relatively trivial, like nicking post, and spoke quietly on his behalf to the policeman,
"As his branch representative, may I ask what the charge is?"
Foolishly, and trying to usurp some authority, the rookie PCSO butted in loudly, "He needs to come with us now sir! After all he could be charged with murder!"
As a result of this perfect example of not engaging brain before opening gob, the whole pub was visibly taken aback. Especially the constable who threw his eyes up in the air and said "Don't be silly Cyril" and addressing Rocky in dulcet tones explained, "They just need to talk to him, he is not under arrest."
Still not satisfied, Rocky bravely offered to accompany Alan. Alan replied calmly "It's alright Rocky, I expect bloody Blake is trying to put me in the frame for one of his pieces of debasement again!"

Rocky had no idea what he was talking about, or who 'bloody Blake' was, but helpfully made sure Alan had his phone number before he was carted away.

After they went, Rocky hoped to throw some light on the matter by enquiring about Blake amongst the remaining posties. No one wanted to proffer an opinion. Although Alan and Rocky were not close, he was furious at the embarrassment the PCSO had subjected his colleague to, especially after coming out with what looked to be a porky in a pub full of inebriated postmen. He communicated this strongly to Shakira whilst relating the incident.

"Oh gawd, it sounds like The New Sheriff in Town has struck again" she explained "or The New Pensioner on the Block as Micky calls him. He loves a drama and thinks he's in charge. We don't know if Alan is connected to any inquiry yet, let alone a murder. Anyway if he has actually been arrested they'll have read his rights and assigned a solicitor, so don't worry."

"Who's Blake?" Rocky asked, but Shakira evaded the question saying it was complicated, only really because it was.

At work, even before she'd taken her coat off, Julian's phone rang. It was Micky and he gave her a message for Julian - "Just tell him they found Blake" he yelled, almost as *she* was at fault. Apart from a sudden universal inability to answer phones, there was an odd atmosphere in the office. She felt like a schoolgirl being sent to Coventry. This made her wary, so when Julian eventually turned up she assumed she was in for some sort of pasting, but he just said,

"Blake was found dead in the river yesterday. He was underneath the terrace, outside The Fisherman's. As far as they could see he had been struck on the head before he drowned" then he muttered as if it was obvious.

"We are going to need to talk to Rocky, Michael!"

Groping for the connecting logic she burbled,

"Rocky is only an acquaintance of Alan's, he does not know much about his private life, I doubt he can tell you anything"

"Then why was he looking for Blake?" he replied sternly,

"Funnily enough, Rocky asked me if I knew who Blake was last night. I evaded the question because I thought it unprofessional to discuss a case with my husband" she lied,"In future I will respond more informatively as you so often seem to need his help these days"
She replied, using satire to cover her shock at the accusing manner in which he spoke about Rocky. She was also irked that her team were behaving like members of Spectre. It occurred to her Julian would make a rubbish Bond-like villain. Nevertheless, when she got home she asked Rocky if he would go and see Micky.
"So do they think Alan is guilty of something then?" he asked,
"We'll I don't know" she muttered, "They asked if you could drop in to clear something up, I probably shouldn't say, but Alan's friend Blake was found floating in the Yare with a head wound"
Rocky just said "Do they think Alan clonked him one on the head?" Then as an afterthought whispered,
"Oh I see, you mean he's dead then?"
"Alan was upstairs with you at the time, and then in custody so I don't know what they are on about. Just pop in and shut him up please darlin'. Oh and they want you to bring in your bike gear, something to do with the scarf, don't ask me what! Micky was ensconced in the depths of Ecins when I left, so he's probably still there"
Micky had already gone when Rocky arrived. Julian kept him waiting, making him nervous. When he was eventually shuffled into the room, without prompting he blurted,
"Alan told me the police were under the impression he had done something stupid that was really down to some bloke called Blake. But I'm sure he wouldn't hurt anyone."
Julian just asked "Rocky, is this your scarf?"
"Yes, well it looks like mine, I lost it in the pub" he replied bemused by the question.
"Thanks for coming in, please may we keep the bike helmet you'll get it back, " he said dismissively, in a manner that curtailed any questions.

This curtness had made Rocky feel even more in the dark. What had his misplaced scarf and an old bike helmet got to do with anything? Julian had grimaced at him as though he was guilty of something. One of the things he did not like about policemen was that they behaved as if everyone else was a villain.

Also being given the run around Shakira assumed Alan must be in some sort of trouble as he was still in custody. She was supposed to be part of this unit, so why was she feeling that wall of silence again. She had been told that Alan had been in the pub with Rocky when Blake was still alive, so she pressed Micky to clarify the events,

"After a heated conversation with Blake" he explained "Alan left The Pumpkin. Blake had another pint there and then pursued him to The Fisherman's Arms to have something out with him. The PCSO had seen Blake go in the pub. But after arresting Alan, they looked down Prince of Wales Road for Blake assuming he had left the pub by the front door. They just thought he had given them the slip and decided to catch up with him later. Now it seems he was killed soon after. He probably went down to the empty bar and wandered outside, where he was belted and thrown in the river where the barman found him the next day." He paused pensively then continued,

"Bizarrely, one witness saw a man lurking around the towpath near the steps before the police came in. Another saw a man of similar description walking down them and hanging around by the gate, but it was definitely not Blake, or Alan for that matter. Being so near Norwich's night spots, Blake's demise was dismissed as the plight of yet another drunk falling in the Yare. As the police had attended the day before they made further enquiries. The P.M. showed up the blunt force trauma. This was indeed a murder but it was hard to imagine it was orchestrated by Alan."

A day later Alan was released, without charge. He had told Micky he had indeed thought Blake, with his record of violence against women, had done away with Mara and put her body bits in two bin bags in close proximity to his doorstep. While he waited in the cell, he had sobered up and seen sense. He realised the bags had been dumped just as close to Blake's door as his. It suddenly became clear to him that his cohort was an unlikely murderer. When Micky had told him Blake had been found dead in the river he was astounded and upset,
"I can't tell him what an idiot I have been now then, can I?" he grizzled "I s'pose he drowned because he fell in the water plastered, did he?" Micky did not answer but changed the subject.
"Tell me about the scarf Alan?" Alan looked at Micky's raised eyebrows and realised he was scuppered,
"Blake found a scarf that belonged to Mara in one of the bags so I knew the body was hers. It had some blood on it so I thought he was completely bonkers when he shoved it in his pocket. That was until he turned up at the works Beano. Then I realised the one Rocky wore under his bike helmet was identical. When Blake arrived, it was tucked inside the helmet on the bar while Rocky was in the Gents. Blake swapped Mara's scarf with Rocky's and scarpered downstairs to drop it the river outside, muttering something about getting me out of trouble. By the time I realised what he was up to the coppers were at the door. In his drink addled brain he assumed I had killed Mara, so he was trying to fit Rocky up. It was a stupid, drunken idea."
He paused and then said calmly,
"I don't know who killed Mara or Blake or what Blake did with Rocky's scarf.I took Mara's out of the helmet before the police came in and found Rocky with it" He took the scarf from his pocket and gave it to Micky
"They gave it back to me without noticing the blood"
"Oh I see!" said Micky mysteriously as if this was big news. So it was Rocky's scarf we found in the bottom bar, did Rocky go downstairs at all?"
"No definitely not, just straight across the bar to the toilet, Blake must have dropped it"

Later, the Forensic Scientific Investigator confirmed not only that the body parts were Mara, but that weirdly they had been frozen, hence the diluted blood. Her head and torso were missing, which was something the press did not know, and blatantly neither did Blake or Alan. Suddenly Shakira had another Eureka moment and shouted excitedly in the direction of a busy Micky who was only vaguely listening.
"Mara's body parts had already been dismembered and frozen, right? The door was fixed, so whoever dragged her in through the back door, presumably her killer, must have opened the front door to unlock the back from inside. Blake had not been near the flat and didn't have keys, neither did Alan."
"I don't understand what you are getting at," piped up Diane almost defensively,
"So who does still have keys?" asked Shakira triumphantly and they both yelled,
"The Caretaker!"
"Oh hell" interrupted Micky, suddenly paying attention, before running out the door after them.
"Tha's a fierce bit of constabulary work" he yelled at Shakira over his shoulder.
When he, Shakira and the two uniforms arrived Howard was acquiescent. Julian arrived with a warrant and cautioned him, which rocketed Howard to launch into a garbled confession, Micky advised him in no uncertain terms, "Shut you up boy, wait 'til we're in the nick!"
Inexplicably he handed Micky a key to a locked room, which he gave to the FCI when she arrived. As soon as she had ushered them out, they gingerly unlocked the door. Walking in they saw a large freezer and the horror of the possible outcome overwhelmed them, as did the smell. Inside the freezer they made the macabre discovery of the woman's head and torso.
By the time a brief had been summoned and having resigned himself to the situation Howard's admissions had become quite articulate,
"Pretending I saw someone running away was stupid. Ada just missed me smashing the glass. It had been an impulsive idea to make Mara come home and it worked.

"Ada had gone off to Bingo and without excusing the absence of a proper council carpenter, I made sure my appearance to repair it was timely. I persuaded Mara to come and wait at my place while I got some tools. She'd had a drink and I thought I could get her to have sex with me this time, well she let everyone else do it with her. When I tried to snog her she pushed me off. So I became more forceful. I still thought she might go for it. Then she started making a racket, so to quieten her I put her headscarf round her mouth but when I pulled it tight, it slipped round her neck, I didn't realise and then I seemed to touch a nerve in the struggle and she just fell, limp. Then I saw she had stopped breathing and gone blue I knew she was gone I didn't mean to, it was a mistake I swear!"
Micky and Julian were unconvinced by this attempt to hide his nefandous nature, especially when Mara's fluids were discovered on his bedding mixed with his semen.
Despite the advice of his barrister, like many narcissistic killers Howard thought he was brighter than the rest of humanity. While languishing on remand, he cooked up a plea of diminished responsibility. His confidence in this erroneous plot led his verbiage to become less guarded and caused him, during an interrogation by special detectives, to spill out a much more lurid account,
"On the first day after, she was still lying in the back room. They came to the door but not inside my flat but I knew I had to get rid of her, so I put her in the bath and cut her up using my old butchery chainmail gloves. It was gruesome but I kept telling myself I had to do it. I kept telling myself I was cutting a piece of beef. I hid the bits in the freezer in black bags and scrubbed everywhere with bleach. The worst bit was slicing through the joints so I could cut the sinew. I was going to cut the middle in half and put it in two bags."
"Wouldn't nearby residents hear the noise and suspect you were up to no good?" one of them enquired,

"Not really. The people upstairs made a hell of a racket here and the druggies bang doors all hours of the night. There was only nosy Ada, and she was out. I had disposed of the gloves and overalls first. Mara's body had been in the freezer a while and no one had been round. I sort of hid my head in the sand because no one had come back. Everyone thought she had just gone off with another bloke and I tried to tell myself no one would bother to look for her now."

Micky and Shakira watched through the glass. One interrogator asked,

"What made you take the bags out?"

"It was when they came round and started asking about the door again. It was totally out of the blue. I had thought it was all done and dusted, so they caught me off guard. As soon as they went I panicked. Her flat was empty and the council told me they were going to re-let it so I was sure them science people had finished. I unlocked her back door then dragged the bags from my place so I could dump them in the middle of the night."

"So what stopped you? Why leave them in her flat? He asked, "I could hear someone in the alley, they hung about for about an hour, and it was almost light by the time the coast was clear. I got spooked and plonked them in her cupboard and ran."

"I went back the next night. The hot weather had caused them to defrost and dribble out onto the lino. I dumped the bags in various industrial bins, early doors and cleaned up. I thought they'd just tip them in the dustcart like they did the gloves and overalls and the council workers would slop a bit of paint over the mess for a new tenant"

"You were seen on CCTV dumping the bags. That was you wasn't it Howard?"

"Yes it was me!" he confessed and eventually went to trial where he pleaded guilty.

Willing as Howard had been to implicate Blake in an attempt to detract from his own butchery. Micky did not think killing him could have been part of his strategy however distorted his moral compass might have been. Apart from that, Howard could not have been anywhere near The Fisherman's Arms when Blake died. Firstly because people saw him in the local shop and around the flats, which was more than a bus ride away from the pub and secondly Blake had no idea that Howard was Mara's killer, so he would not have confronted him. Howard would not have killed Blake, he had no motive.

Chapter 7, The Guv'nor

Shakira left people in no doubt about her animosity toward Frazer from the get go. The feeling was mutual. The misogynist was astounded by a woman who knew her own mind and what's more, had the audacity to express an opinion. He could not conceive of a woman who could not be bullied into submission and who made it crystal' that she would not tolerate his sexism and particularly his racism, under any circumstances.

When one of his many bigoted remarks had caused her to march out of his newly acquired premises vowing never to return in his lifetime, he took her display of bravery as that of a fool. Not only did his inability to intimidate her present an unknown quantity, but he had no idea how prophetic her promise was to be.

Still infuriated the next day when trying to top up a nasty hangover, Frazer caught a glimpse of Rocky who, completely by chance, had the misfortune to be driving past the pub while Frazer wobbled about outside. Fulfilling his reputation as an aggressive drunk whose temper was out of control, Frazer left his girlfriend alone to manage the bar and got in his van. Already the worse for wear, he tailgated Rocky to his destination, which was his own home.

Accustomed to his hazardous behaviour on the road and his general recklessness even when not at the wheel of 3.5 tons of metal, Rocky gave him a wide berth and kept his cool, behaving as if he had not noticed he was being pursued by a drunken nutcase. Frazer had still been in hot pursuit when Rocky reached his front gate. With an abrupt change of tack, he pulled up sharply, causing Frazer to stand on the brakes. Rocky slammed his own car door and brazenly marched toward Frazer whose aggressive bravado as he slung opened his door and leapt to his feet suddenly left Frazer sober and face to face with his nemesis. He stood helpless for a moment while Rocky breathed genuine venom in his face,

"Come on then sunshine, bring it on!" Rocky challenged, Predictably, Frazer had sheepishly returned to the safety of his vehicle and fled at top speed back to his drinking house.

Frazer's far from serendipitous arrival from a small town near Hartlepool, prompted Rocky to dub him The Monkey-Hanger. Frazer's motley crew, an entourage of sycophantic benefit cheats, unfamiliar with a world north of Kings Lynn, were bewildered by the term. They couldn't comprehend why it was a moniker their out-of-control gang-master found so hard to tolerate. In fact to be on the safe side, it was best not to mention his roots altogether. A band of citizens ill equipped for life, or a tax-paying job, did not want a Taurus semi-automatic pistol pointing in their direction. That is if he had actually owned one. His violent moods, his incompetence and his offensive jokes, soon meant his business was in trouble.

Predictably, the apprentice womaniser, although still in training with ladies of the night, began regarding his live-in punch-bag Amy as an encumbrance. Indeed they were both trapped in this unholy union. For a good while she had been forbidden to leave the premises and was to blame for his every mishap.

Desperately alone, she had confided in local women but despite their best intentions and the untimely appearance of the strong arm of the law enquiring after Amy's welfare, just put the cat amongst the pigeons.

Eventually the holding company threatened Frazer with notice, unless things improved. Like any gambler he upped the ante and with the aid of the odd fairy-tale, continued to borrow substantial amounts of money.

"I've got another two pubs and a chip shop up north you know" he lied unconvincingly to the hoi polloi "My cousin runs one for me and my friend the other," he rumbled on.

Actually his elder brother owned a pub, the younger a chip shop. Frazer had relinquished ownership of the other pub to his business partner, before the bailiffs turned up.

His family were not party to his ill thought out promises and had been dutifully forwarding his unopened mail, thus exacerbating his dilemma.

Arrogance and his state of mind left him without the wherewithal for a logical strategy. Instead, he had left the bewildered Amy in the pub and returned home with bogus promises and tales of wealth from his successful ventures in Norwich, in order to embezzle more 'loans' from the naively greedy. The only lucrative scheme he ever had a hand in was dealing coke before some heavy duty rivals warned him off.
On his trip back up north, he stopped at a pub in Leeds. There he bumped into some illegal immigrants professing to be from Lithuania. Their deception was wasted on him as any ethnic distinction was way beyond his capabilities. They persuaded him to help them buy and sell their product, illegal vodka. Before distributing it to a smattering of the less well informed and not so sharp proprietors of Norfolk and Hartlepool he thought he better sample some himself. Already a hazardous drinker, he did not recognise the side effects of a moonshine made with methanol.
His predators had masked the chemical taste with cola, and the effects began aggravating his already serious health problems. By the time he had made enough profit to return to Norfolk, his skin was yellow. Whatever his sins, sadly this slippery slope had left him without a trusted ally to persuade him to stop.
By this time Amy was no longer able to convince herself that he was that knight in shining armour who really did love her. Slowly the rusty penny dropped and she had returned to live with her Mum. Frazer had tried to juggle his little empire before it came crashing down. The pub rapidly slipped through his fingers like sand.
With no collateral to buy beer he flogged the fixtures and fittings to buy more iffy vodka, telling the company their assets had disappeared in a series of burglaries, while he was in hospital. Eventually he posted the pubs keys through the letter box and walked away. To save face with his new found cohorts he continued to distribute their noxious bootleg elsewhere.

Having ingratiated himself with its manager, Frazer had begun to hang about in The George, behaving as if he owned the place. He had hooked up with an older woman he met there, Evelyn. The unfortunate carer for the elderly was in the middle of a shift when she eventually got the news of Frazer's demise and although it had come as no surprise, it made her very sad. Shakira had been familiar with more of the events in this morbid story than were contained within the laborious notes. Given the dearth of any deep exploration, the Coroner's verdict of 'misadventure' seemed surprisingly enlightened, so she wondered what could be added to this sorry tale.

Initially, Nick had persuaded Julian there had been gaps in the finer details of this woeful chronicle of events. He had argued that the forensic pathologist had been bothered by the bang on his forehead. Originally it had been assumed a fall against a tree had knocked him out and along with the booze and his liver precipitated his demise. Nick had asserted that he could also have been hit with a blunt instrument, although there had been no indication that anyone else was present when he passed out behind the bin.

Micky and Shakira first went to see Evelyn. She was obviously reluctant to re-visit Frazer's hardly unexpected but painful expiry.

"He was found dead in the car park," she related bluntly "I did try to stop him drinking, but he wouldn't listen."

After the usual condolences, Micky commiserated,

"We are sure there was nothing more you could have done for him. There are just a couple of points we need to re-visit, if it's alright with you."

She nodded in assent,

"When Dom found him," Micky continued, "nobody could fathom why a man who could barely walk had gone out so far in the pouring rain just for a cigarette. There was a covered shelter with seats nearby. It was, by all accounts, a miserable day in which he had been particularly ill and unsteady on his feet. Dom pointed out that even smokers who went out the front door, seldom strayed far from the pub, even in more clement weather. You knew his habits, can you make sense of it?"

Evelyn spoke slowly recalling Dom's words,
"It did strike me as odd at the time, in that weather and in the dark." She paused and then struggling to remember the events, "Now let me recall what Dom said" she began" Frazer had been chatting to some builder. They went out the side door towards the smoking room and Frazer had a rolly behind his ear. It was twilight even then. Hours later, Dom was collecting pots. He checked the room and garden which were empty and then went out to the car-park by the front door. Neither man came back to the bar, so everyone assumed they had come through the pub unnoticed, and gone home. As he bent down to pick up a glass, he caught sight of Frazer's feet sticking out from behind a recycling bin. When he got closer he recognised him and saw he was unconscious, until the ambulance came he said it was hard to tell if he was still alive".
"Did they tell you he had banged his head?" asked Micky. She thought for a moment and then remembered,
"Yes, um someone said he had splinters of wood and bark in the cut on his forehead, it seems he had knocked himself out on a tree or something, he was always tripping over."
"Do you know who the other bloke could be Evelyn?" asked Micky
"Well none of us could place him. Dom heard them talk about building and Frazer had been in the trade. Frazer was always chatting to potential business associates, but they found no recent calls or new numbers on his mobile. The hospital found a bit of money and his bank cards so he wasn't robbed. Frazer had been ill since I met him. When Dom rang me I assumed his poor pickled liver had finally given up the ghost."
"As far as we know it did" Micky said gently, "but we just need to make sure of all the details, you have been very helpful. I'm sorry to bring this all up again, we'll leave you in peace" he ushered Shakira towards the door.
Evelyn and Dom's record of events were consistent so on the way back Shakira asked him who was next on his list.
"D'you fancy a trip to Greatham." He enquired.
She thought for a moment and then said "Mmm, Yes, I know it, it's near Hartlepool. Is that where Amy lives?"

Shakira was unusually quiet on the way. Micky asked her if she was alright. Shakira realised she should make her situation clear,
"If I seem apprehensive it's because Amy and I did not really like each other. Like Frazer she was amused by winding me up with unnecessary and random racism. Although she did confide in me once about his temper. He often belted her you know"
Micky tried to reassure her,
"Don't worry, just keep your head down and take notes. I will deal with any animosity."
Shakira's assertion was spot on. Amy strongly vocalised that she was miffed that her husband's girlfriend knew he was dead before she did, and directed her answers to Micky's questions accusingly at Shakira. She seemed to blame everyone else in the world for their failures and Frazer's demise, especially his enemy Rocky, who she talked about as if he practiced black magic. Micky tried to nip this in the bud,
"Shakira's only role in this enquiry is to take notes, Amy. Since Rocky had no recent contact with Frazer, he has no relevance to the investigation. I am the one who has been asked to come and talk to you"
Seemingly oblivious to his statement, she rumbled on,
"Everyone who upsets Rocky seems to come to a bad end, I mean look at your neighbour" She volleyed this in Shakira's direction again,
"He died not long after falling out with your old man!"
Shakira grimaced at Micky who nodded at her to indicate she could reply to her ludicrous mumbo-jumbo.
"My neighbour died of a heart attack Amy!" Shakira said gently,
"Well Rocky said it was korma!" Amy fired back.
For a moment Shakira thought this was the beginning of some racist diatribe, until both members of Amy's audience cottoned on.
"Do you mean Karma?" Micky said. Shakira recognised Rocky's explanation for both deaths. It was true he had not cared for either person.

"We were both very sorry!" she fibbed diplomatically, but this unexpected sympathy from the opposition wrong footed her enough to calm her down. With a little stern coercion from Micky she started being cooperative,

Amy described with familiarity The George's regular bar exhibits, many of whom also bedecked the furniture her own establishment. She was positive this northern chap frequented neither.

Both women had agreed Frazer was not short of enemies. During the odd drunken moment of paranoia when laced with Dutch courage he threatened to shoot members of his apparent rivals, especially Rocky. But neither had ever seen the much referred to pistol.

"He had a baseball bat which he took to the George. It's probably in Dom's beer garden somewhere", Amy said almost helpfully

"Thanks Amy, that's really useful. I expect it's still there somewhere" Shakira pointed out warmly.

As they left Micky praised her observation,

"Good point. It's a blunt instrument possibly used in a crime that is still outstanding, I'll get uniform out there," Micky assured her as they made their way back through Hartlepool to The Harry, Frazer's brother's pub.

After some introductions, Frazer's Mum, Doris gave them some family background,

"Frazer Senior, brought us here from Glasgow. He was a hard working builder and left all the boys some money to start a business each. My eldest Marvin was actually Frazer's step-brother, because he looked different they call him cousin. My middle son Killen with the chip shop, nearly lost it to Frazer's creditors.

"From a very young age he had his father's 'liking for a wee swallie' she said in her genteel Aberdeen brogue.

"Frazer said he had put money in The Burton round the corner. Frazer blamed Joe, who runs it, for his loss of capital," Doris continued honestly "but Joe continued to make a go of it after Frazer went to Norwich so I don't know what happened there"

"The thing was," said Marvin "Our Frazer couldn't be told .He had no idea how to run a pub, he was good at sitting in the bar blaked, so I'm not surprised he and Amy couldn't hack it!"
"She couldn't bloody cook either!" Killen said. They all laughed, but in an affectionate sort of way. Micky talked to Killen in the gents and he added,
"It may not seem so to you DS Saint but I know Frazer wasn't perfect but he was my brother and I loved him, but he *was* all talk. He'd always got some scheme going and he often made out he'd got a gun, but I never seen it. He used to keep an old rounders' bat in his room, but he never used it, well not as far as I know."
"But he was prone to violence?" Asked Micky
"Well you're a copper, you must have looked up his form!"
Micky and Shakira popped into The Burton to meet Joe. He confirmed their suspicions that Frazer's investment had been a figment of his imagination.
"Money burned a hole in his pocket!" he recalled affectionately.
Shakira noted that Joe didn't resemble Dom's description of the stranger either and he had little to add. In fact the trip had bought them very little more information, but she did conclude that if someone had walloped Frazer, it was unlikely to be anyone they had met here. All these people seemed to have accepted his shortcomings without malice.
Meanwhile Julian, Liz and Nick with his clipboard had been back to speak to Dom in The George,
"It was obvious he would need more than his usual taxi when I found him in the garden." He said
"He just looked unconscious. I put down the glasses and ran straight to the bar to phone 999, my mobile was by the till." His wife nodded in agreement adding,
"He was only out there for five minutes before he came back in a panic, shouting for an ambulance"
"What was this builder like?" said Julian
"If he *was* a builder, I can only vaguely remember him" he muttered,

"Northern, average height wearing a green parka. He had a scruffy beard and was probably in his forties. He wore driving gloves, he put them on the bar when he came in but he didn't have a car with him. I watched him put them back on when they went out for a cigarette".

He thought for a moment and then said, "I don't remember who else saw him and I was on my own when they went out and it was quiet" he said defensively.

"Ah yes! There was one other thing", said Dom. "I did not notice with all the kerfuffle, but someone had taken off the padlock on the back gate. I did not see the scruffy chap come through the bar so it could have been him I suppose"

Maybe Frazer was belted with bolt cutters Julian thought. Dom's original description along with a couple of others had been pretty consistent, except the gloves, he had not mentioned gloves before. Picking up on his other comment he asked, "Why do you say, *if* he was a builder?"

"Well I realise they were talking about building, but he didn't look like someone who had worked on a site recently to me, and he did not dress like it either "said Dom "it's a shame someone had nicked the CCTV"

"If Frazer had trouble walking, was he carrying a stick?" Nick asked intelligently.

"Not him" said Dom, "a stick would have looked weak. He used to borrow this old girl's mobility scooter sometimes, when he was really bad, but not that day. Don't get me wrong he was really ill and we all knew he was not long for this world!"

Back at the station, the pathologist addressed a team meeting,

"As part of the review into the death of Mr Frazer Archibald Argyle, I have been asked to review the Post-Mortem results with a view to possible foul-play. I have been asked to look at three possible contributing factors to his organ failure. Firstly, the high quantity of alcohol, secondly the advanced stage of his liver cirrhosis and thirdly, the cause of his head injury. Although all three contributed I am now satisfied that the head injury was the cause of death. I am now certain that the splinters of wood in the wound were from two sources. Some was indeed consistent with bark from a tree trunk, but the other was some sort of varnished maple. But Forensics found no blood near the body or on any nearby trees."
"So we need to search again for a possible outstanding weapon. Whatever hit his head must be covered in blood" Shakira pointed out.
"Well that's not for me to determine, but yes a blunt instrument was a possibility!"
Shakira asked Micky if they could go and have another look at the George as she had a theory. She began to put it to him while he drove there,
"What if Frazer upset the bloke out in the garden. They were both drunk so any fisticuffs would have sent him flying. If Frazer was out cold the bloke would want to get away before he got nicked, especially if he had belted him with something after he had fallen on a tree".
"Possibly, still very iffy" concurred Micky sarcastically,
"If there was a weapon, he could have used it to smash the padlock and get out the gate so he did not have to go back indoors. It was quiet in the bar but the music would have covered the noise. It was dark so could have carried him out of the gate across to the bin, he would have just looked drunk. He could have taken the weapon with him and dumped it nearby"
Dom unlocked the gate so Shakira could retrace the man's steps. Suddenly she walked quickly around the edge of the car-park. She was masked by bushes. On the other side of the pub there was a dingy alley. Next to it was a gap between a shed and a fence.

"Did they look down here!" she asked, pointing to a small space less than a foot wide. Micky had to shine a torch down the gap even in daylight, it was overgrown with weeds but she squeezed herself with difficulty between the shed and the fence and reached down.

"There's something here" she said, reaching behind her to effect better purchase. Eventually some old boy among the spectators, handed her his stick and she reached the handle of bloodstained rounders' bat"

"Wow you clever girl!" shouted Micky, as he took it from her gingerly, even in his latex disposables. "Err, I mean good work Ms Browning" he corrected himself.

They found blood on a tree by the back gate. Forensics concluded that not only had Frazer been struck with the bat because his blood was still on it, but so had someone else. The only fingerprints matched Frazer's but there was two sources of DNA. When Shakira enquired who it belonged to, they all did their mysterious act again. Irked by this she mentioned it to Nick who knew all the station goss.

He said "I got the impression they could not identify the other blood, but while only Frazer bashed his head on the tree, two people were struck with the bat. You have probably opened up a can of worms, but that's hardly your fault!"

Chapter 8 Dead Pool

At painfully early doors, and with scant clarification not to mention lame excuses, Micky crammed Shakira and Nick into a waiting police wagon and dragged them off to Great Yarmouth Investigation Centre.

While he and Inspector Tom McPherson briefly indulged in a load of fatuous office-speak about 'cooperation of forces' and 'joined up policing' at the cop shop, Nick and Shakira were thrust into the capable hands of PC Yvonne Petrov.

Yvonne's was one of the Force's go getters. This was immediately obvious by her need to power dress, even when in uniform. A perfectionist with a potent penchant for promotion - not to mention positive persuasion. A master of delegation and manipulation, which her naturally sunshiny personality enabled her to achieve. Nevertheless, her colleagues were terrified to ruffle her uniform, let alone her feathers.

Her partner Nadia Shah's light skin and western style betrayed little of her ethnicity. Her demeanour similarly conveyed a hankering for management status. She had always been slightly more approachable than Yvonne, with an innate warmness and humility which thinly veiled a ferocious hunger for moral justice.

While the newbies comfortably languished in the hubbub of the noisy call-centre which was reputedly the crux of the town's Community policing, Yvonne picked up a call Tom had patched through. Despite the outward pretence of some mundane procedure, Nick and Shakira suspected a conspiracy was afoot, so it was curiosity that gave them the incentive to accept the invitation to accompany Yvonne to The Coastal Holiday Camp. Yvonne effected a version of charades in an attempt to extricate Nadia from a difficult phone call, so she could accompany them. She signalled a promise to catch them up.

As they approached The Reception, Shakira had feelings of nostalgia and couldn't help thinking British Holiday Camps had become shadows of their former selves.

Yvonne and her fledglings were greeted by The Camp's Manager whose phone call had expressed concern about yet another HSE report that had been unceremoniously plonked on his desk. It informed him of a continuance of a probe into the pool's drowning tragedy last year. He had previously been led to believe the whole thing was done and dusted, but this document indicated otherwise. Although slightly addled by the MOJ'S renewed interest, he was keen to comply. It included a forensic report blatantly way beyond the comprehension of everyone present, especially when Shakira stated the obvious, a dubious talent of hers, at the best of times.
"What's a spectroscopy when it's at home?" she asked reading upside down.
After an embarrassing pause, and a room of blank faces, Guy interjected, anxious to facilitate an evasion of the question,
"I have collated the transcripts of all the procedures we have applied since the accident."
She heard him fumbling as they left.
Shakira whispered to Nick "It never hurts to cover your back"
Despite the hint of sarcasm, Yvonne smiled and nodded in agreement in her direction.
For more than twenty years, Camp Managers, Guy and Sonia Riley had left their North London home in early spring and returned in early autumn, in order to run The Camp's chaotic Activities and Entertainment. Being so close to retirement, the last thing they had expected or needed on their watch, had been this unfortunate disaster.
Guy was a dapper, always suited and booted man, with immaculate dark but greying hair and a broad cockney accent. In contrast Sonia, had no perceptible dialect and although conventionally dressed, she always looked slightly dishevelled. He was very much the showman, while she ran everything else. Sonia may have been a formidable woman, but she treated her staff like family.

While Yvonne talked to Guy and Sonia, Nadia arrived and introduced herself properly to Shakira and Nick and handed each of them a printout of all the relevant documents. They were hastily dispatched to mercilessly interrogate the unsuspecting Activity Assistants, Coaches and Lifeguards with the blessing of the management. Enjoying the freedom to organise their own workload the rookies first enlisted the assistance of "Cheerful Chas" the Activities Manager.

Shakira thought he looked a bit like a deck chair in his white and blue striped jacket, reminiscent of the old bluecoats. After an exchange of pleasantries, Shakira asked him if he would mind showing them the pool. As they walked she told him how impressed she was with the new chalets. She pointed out their stilts made them resemble exotic dwellings in Thailand, rather than the ramshackle concrete Nissan hut's tolerated by the camp inmates of yesteryear.

Given his age, Chas was probably a leftover bluecoat from that time.

"Of course, we would like to help in any way we can," he said, changing the subject. He ushered them into an area next to the peaceful water.

"The pool does not open until nine" his voice intimated a certain relief at the calm before the storm.

"The victim of the incident was a woman called Agnes." he reflected sombrely.

"She was an adult with Downs Syndrome, of comparatively high ability, and who was well aware of the possible dangers of deep water. I mention this as a point of interest, because she had never gone into into the main pool without Jane, before this time.

"The first inkling of her difficulties was proven to be too late. She was already unconscious when a swimmer started to rescue her. He had caught her by the ankle when he realised her body was still, and her head was underwater. With a tighter grip under her arms, he athletically bounced from the water to a sitting position on the pool's edge and lifted her out gently, his feet still dangling in the water. The lifeguards ran to his aid immediately and gave her CPR. Nobody had seen where or when she had entered the pool, or how she had slipped under, unnoticed."

His narrative revealed not only that he was close to Agnes but probably present at the time.

As it filled with early swimmers, Nick chatted to a couple of green stripy Lifeguards who were very cooperative. He noticed impressively, even while in conversation, they kept a constant eye on their charges. He could see nothing about the operation of this lido that gave an indication of laxity. Chas had asserted that the prevention of injury to campers was paramount and that seemed to pan out.

Instead of the reluctance they had expected, Chas and his team seemed almost too obliging but then it was unofficial, and their inquisitors were only students. Referring to the notes Shakira asked him,

"Who was this couple she spoke to in the locker room?"

"Well this was curious too" continued Chas "as no one recognised them as being local, or understood what the devil Agnes was doing in there. Her carer had been totally unaware she had returned to The Camp. She never changed at the pool and had no business messing about by the lockers.

"Sorry, I'm not being very lucid, Jane is my cousin and she was Agnes' guardian. When Agnes got bored with swimming, Jane would give her a towel and flip flops and walk her back to her care home next door where she would stay. The whole episode was such a tragedy, Agnes was such a popular person. I had known her for a long time and Jane is devastated. No one blamed Jane for what happened, but she seems to have taken it upon herself to feel guilty."

Shakira was wondering if it was Chas who was feeling culpable. After all, he was in charge of The Lifeguards.

Commiserating with him she said,

"Losing someone so close is painful so both of you are bound to feel hurt."

To qualify this officially, she helpfully read from the notes

"No fault was found with her professional caring skills. The authorities have expressed no reason for her to take the blame for what seemed, by all accounts, to be a sad accident. The cuts and bruises Agnes sustained were consistent with the first aid administered by and in the pool."

He replied slightly defensively,

"Yes the Health and Safety's only recommendation was that vulnerable adults should always be accompanied when the pool is busy. Naturally, this had irritated Jane as apart from being blindingly obvious, it was the first time one of her residents had ever ventured in on their own, especially one who she thought was still at home. In addition, no one saw Agnes being cajoled or pushed as had been inferred, either. The HSE were suitably satisfied with our procedures and like your coroner, agreed the accident was not negligence but misadventure."
He paused thoughtfully and then with his voice affected by his sadness, he said from the heart,
"We still have no idea how she ended up in the deep end. If you have reason to think there was any funny business, we would like to be the first to know." recovering from his visible anguish he suggested decisively,
"You will want to speak to Jane, I have to stay here but I'm sure she would be happy to help in any way she can, I'll give her a ring"
He was still talking to her on the phone when they arrived next door. Jane was already standing at the gate. The three of them sat on a bench in the warmth of the sun and a housekeeper put tea and biscuits on a nearby table.
"I hope you don't mind chatting outside" she said accounting for the al-fresco tea party,
"We try not to disrupt the residents by introducing strangers, anyway they would only drive you mad asking endless questions."
"Agnes was a little ray of sunshine, she had a wicked sense of humour and a talent for making people feel at ease in her company. If she couldn't do something she would throw her eyes up in the air as if to say "Here we go again" She used to point with her thumb to indicate the direction she was headed in, so you could follow her.
Then as if awoken from a dream she said "Sorry you want me to tell you about her circumstances"
"Yes please" Shakira said lowering her voice reverently,
Jane obliged as she poured the tea,

"Her dad has never been traced and her mum Joan, died when she was just fourteen, long before we came here. I lived nearby so it was easy for me to look after Agnes while Joan was working. When she became ill, Joan had appointed me as Agnes's guardian before she passed away. When I started a live in job at the home Agnes came with me as a resident. Although she has family in Norwich somewhere, they were not interested and never came to see her. Her Uncle Duane and a few others turned up for the funeral, hoping she left some money I suppose!"

Shakira got the impression Jane felt that the family did not have time for Agnes because of her disability.

She went on,

"I only knew Joan briefly. All Agnes could remember is that she had been a solicitor, was very kind, and liked to drink wine. She died when comparatively young, but rumour has it she left Agnes quite a bit of money. Joan's solicitors are also executors of Agnes's will so I presume her family will be put out of their misery soon enough." Almost justifying her last statement she added,

"I have turned over all her expenditure accounts and bank records, she never spent all her benefits because I spoiled her. I expect her relations will get what's left but I didn't care whether she had money or not, because I was her friend. I just thought it was a crying shame that her blood relations never came to see how she was."

Jane had kept a copy of a video made of Agnes's funeral, which Shakira asked to borrow and promised to return to her personally. They thanked her and Shakira said,

"We better go back to the camp before I get Nick in trouble again."

Fortunately Chas had told Nadia where they were. She met them outside the gate and drove them back to Yarmouth, where Micky was waiting to take them home. On the way home Shakira asked Micky if they could continue examining the circumstances around Agnes's misfortune as long as they promised not to rattle anyone's cage.

Delighted that they were both so interested, he agreed to request their return the next day. When Micky emailed Nadia and Yvonne and asked if they minded 'baby-walking' again, Yvonne said Nadia was busy and she could only accommodate them in the afternoon.

He suggested they spend the morning researching the notes, viewing the video of the funeral and the CCTV retained from the pool that afternoon. The video excited her curiosity as in amongst the mourners she caught a glimpse of someone she recognised well. Her old neighbour, who had briefly occupied the house adjoining theirs.

"I was friendly with a woman called Sharon who came to live next door" she explained to Nick "and soon after the man who was at Agnes's funeral, Duane, moved in with her",

"We were wary of him from the get go. If we bumped into him in the pub he was usually consorting with people we would prefer to avoid. We would still greet him politely with the customary nod, but try and sit somewhere else. Sharon had told us he was the father of the child she was very pregnant with, although he kept insisting to all his mates that it wasn't his.

"One evening we heard him come in, off his head as usual. There was a lot of banging and crashing about and then a lot of screaming. Rocky was concerned for Sharon's welfare and looked through a gap in the fence to see if she was in trouble. The kids were in the back garden crying and hysterical. We could see her trying to escape the mayhem, but before she could get away, Duane held her against the back door frame while repeatedly smashing it against her pregnant belly, as if he was deliberately trying to harm the baby.

"As soon as Rocky yelled at him over the fence, he shoved her in the garden and locked her out. We heard him run through the house, slamming the front door behind him. Rocky climbed over and lifted the kids over the fence to me, then helped Sharon over.

Rocky was well aware that ringing the police would have only aggravated the situation if Duane came back, so we bedded them all down in the front room and Rocky insisted she should get an injunction the next morning. I don't know if she did, but Duane never returned."

"Did *you* ever see him again Shakira?" Nick asked

"He started reappearing around Norwich much later on. Rocky and I would say hello to him, but he had enough sense to keep his distance. I heard he'd hooked up with someone else and had more bloody kids with her"

Then Nick started checking the CCTV while Shakira read over the notes, not paying him much attention. There was something about the forensics that bothered her. What were the marks on her shoulders, were they scratches or thumbprints?

"That's Agnes isn't it!" he shouted excitedly "You can just see her curly dyed hair by the pool, she's talking to someone out of the picture"

Shakira said "Sorry, can you wind it back? I was miles away." then later she concurred,

"Oh yes, there she is!"

Nick interrupted triumphantly "and there *he* is!"

"Who?" Shakira muttered missing the point.

"Uncle Duane!" said Nick. "Look, she is talking to someone by the pool, who keeps pulling her away from the camera, and that balding head belongs to the man at Agnes's funeral" he observed smugly.

"Brilliant" said Shakira, now taking notice,

"Wow that is definitely Duane, Nick. Micky said you were observant".

In the afternoon Yvonne identified Uncle Duane as a miscreant currently shacked up with a girl called Cindy, somewhere near The Avenues. She even managed to locate her photo in her rogue's gallery. Not only did she attend the funeral with Duane, but more importantly she was with him and Agnes by the pool. Nadia and Yvonne were impressed.

Nick and Shakira went with Nadia to a meeting to show the CCTV and video to the Camp Asisstants but no one could really remember Duane or Cindy aggravating Agnes. Meanwhile, Yvonne and a PCSO talked to Jane. She was well acquainted with Duane but did not remember seeing either of them that day.

Just as they were all leaving, a security guard appeared and beckoned them back to the camp saying he had some important information about the incident, but wanted to speak in confidence. He ushered them into an empty chalet and explained,

"One of the volunteers Will, called me to the locker room. He complained a woman was upsetting Agnes. I had seen the three of them talking by the pool. Will thought she was just a local 'spare changer' but I had stopped them pestering Agnes before.

"I insisted the woman left the pool and followed her out to make sure, I intended to find Jane while Agnes was with Will, but as soon as I left the locker room I came upon her boyfriend, Duane and some other bloke squabbling close to the water. Before it got physical I asked the other chap to leave the area and watched him go into a nearby chalet. He looked as if he had a drink on him and could do with a kip. I assumed he was residing there as he had a key. Once Duane had calmed down I let him follow his girlfriend to the ballroom.

"When I returned to the locker room. Will had sent Agnes home. The whole episode seemed like something and nothing and because of Agnes's accident later that afternoon I forgot about it until I wrote my weekly report".

"Later that evening I was detailed to work in the ballroom and blow me, the same pair were at it again. The scruffy bloke grabbed Duane by the shoulders from behind. There was a nasty scuffle. One of the punters reported seeing a blade afterwards. Duane and his girlfriend left with no trouble. The other nuisance was drunk and aggressive so I assisted a colleague in ejecting him from the site. We assumed they had all been searched at the door but no one was sure, so to be truthful we don't know if he was tooled up or not."

"OK, we'll look into it", promised Yvonne.

"That was not the weirdest thing though" he continued "as we were hauling the drunk out of the ballroom, he slurred something about getting Duane nicked for drowning the old girl, so he couldn't upset his mate again."

The next morning Nick said,

"I don't know Duane like you do Shakira but let's suppose it wasn't an unfortunate mishap and someone held her under. If he was in line for bit of dosh, I can't see a better motive from anyone else. We already know Duane is a bully and he and his very suggestible girlfriend suddenly turned up just before Agnes drowned. They were the last people to be seen with her. I know the pathologist agreed her injuries could have been sustained by bashing against the sides, or by people banging into her. He said it was just as viable that she was held underwater causing the bruising on her shoulders."

Shakira agreed adding,

"It's true Cindy has the profile of a victim, even more than her predecessor, but any threat of violence from Duane could have persuaded her to back him up. She may not have assisted the actual drowning just in covering it up later. In any case, a bit of folding money seems to create a remarkable change in people's moral compass."

Nick chimed in,

"It would be good if someone had interviewed this other boil on the arse of humanity as well. I'd like to know what hand he had in all of this and if they knew each other, especially if he was shanked up."

Back in Yarmouth, by labelling the drunken stranger the villain of the piece, Nadia was able to chat to Duane, without his concern. Yvonne spoke to Cindy to see if their accounts tallied. They both insisted they left the pool area for the ballroom and said goodbye to Agnes as she left the camp.

As Shakira knew her, she and Nick went to see Sharon. Her opinion was unexpected.

"I would prefer never to see Duane's ugly face again and there is no question that he is violent. If you are asking me if he was capable of really harming Agnes, actually I don't think so."

She paused for thought before continuing,

"The thing is Duane was always tapping Agnes for summink and been warned off by Jane several times. She even refused to give Agnes her own money when he was about. If Agnes wanted to get rid of him, she always used to promise him something in her will, but he never took her seriously"

Shakira made a suggestion, during a call to Nadia and Yvonne, that if the CPS thought Agnes had been the victim of a dirty deed, they would need all the evidence, including a copy of her will. Yvonne's Sergeant said she would get one of her inspectors to speak to the executors and told her not to let the interns 'meddle' anymore. This was the behaviour Shakira had come to expect from the constabulary. Someone who she had never met, berating her hard work, while getting all the brownie points. It transpired, however, that Duane's bequest did not even warrant an invite to attend the reading. In fact, as many people who knew him intimated, he was not the sharpest knife in the box and it had never occurred to him that his niece might have inherited a tidy sum. He had only been interested in scrounging her benefit. There was no question in Shakira's mind that Duane was guilty of domestic abuse and certainly he could browbeat people who got in his bad books, but he clearly had no idea Agnes had any serious money. This meant he had no motive to do her harm, let alone drown her in the pool. Perhaps the whole thing had been an accident after all.

Jane had assumed she had been asked to attend the reading of Agnes's will as her appointee. The most she expected was a trinket. Actually Jane was there because secretly Agnes left her almost everything she had, and that turned out to be a good few bob. It was Duane who got the trinket. After all she did promise him.

Agnes didn't comprehend why people thought they needed lots of money, so she left him something she thought more valuable, because he liked it. There was a picture on her bedroom wall he had often admired. It was of the two of them playing on Yarmouth beach when they were little. Cindy put it on the mantle-piece.

Chapter 9 Builder's Bum

Reggie Adams was more a gang-master than a building contractor. If he had his way he would have owned a row of chicken sheds housing Eastern Europeans like the real slave labour merchants. He was reputed to be an ace bricklayer, but no one could actually remember seeing him lift a trowel and all his recruitment was done in the pub. He worked on his swarthy appearance which, he had convinced himself, along with the fake tan and dark glasses gave him an exciting image of an exotic villain. He was undeniably not local, but his background was more Southend than Saracen and his supposed camaraderie with London gangsters was more than embellished in places.

His recent split with his wife, Sam, and their two little girls, had etched a noticeable wound on his psyche. Work on the conversion of an asylum, enabled him to purchase, (at mate's rates natch) one of the flats. Dwellings miraculously transformed from someone's psychiatric nightmare to a des res. This unsuccessful attempt at reconciliation with his estranged family, resulted in half of his residence being shrouded in dust-sheets. Sometimes Sam would be around for a while, appearing in the pub with him and the kids, then suddenly disappear off the scene equally quickly. Shakira got the sense that Sam had seen money as his only attribute and making a fast buck had undoubtedly been his area of expertise.

Reggie's frequent indulgence in drunken belligerence and his blatant coke habit would not have made him easy to live with. That said, domestic violence had not reared its ugly head as one of his imperfections so far. Moreover his wandering eye seemed mainly to be borne of Sam's see-sawing. For a man like Reggie, not being able to keep hold of a woman he obviously adored was like a kick in the balls.

Rocky and Shakira had watched Reggie holding forth in various establishments, giving them a fair inkling of the man's character. Rocky regarded any coke-head as a liability, but he had always been pleasant enough to Reggie whilst keeping a prudent distance. Anyway Rocky's bricklayer mate, Pint Pot, had regular work with Reggie and he did not wish to rock the boat.

Presently, Reggie had little pockets of interest all over Norwich but unfortunately most of the profits ended up going up his snout. At this juncture, observant Shakira had surmised that one occupation would shortly supersede the other.

When work had started to dry up it had become a struggle to solicit new contracts. He touted for business further out, leading him to ply his trade away from his comfort zone. As he manoeuvred himself away from Norwich, he started to knock back some of his 'brickies'.He may have intended to 'weigh them in' eventually, but withholding wages was a foolhardy stratagem in the building game. There was always the distinct possibility your previous personnel might suddenly materialise on the next site.

As his list of local creditors expanded, so did his unreliable reputation. Finally, having conceded that rekindling his marriage was a nonstarter, he moved even further afield. Occasionally he would erroneously bump into Rocky and Shakira, usually in some out of the way venue, with different women in tow, popping up in places like Sea Palling or Cromer. He would sneak away embarrassed as soon as he was spotted.

Eventually his appearances were so infrequent he even stopped being a topic of local gossip.

Pint Pot became one of Reggie's cash-flow casualties. Tagging along as enforcer, streetwise Rocky tracked the errant subby down, when he and Pint Pot caught up with him in a village pub. A while back, Reggie had started a false and spurious rumour spawned only by his own ego, that Rocky had loaned him a huge wedge. He was now painfully aware of his mistake. The hoi-polloi would have assumed Rocky was a victim in his own right and any ensuing fisticuffs would have been his own fault. So Reggie sensibly offered no resistance and put his hand in his pocket straight away, with the promise of another 'monkey' provided Pint Pot kept schtum about his location. That being agreed, they returned to Norwich where Pint Pot took Rocky's advice not to flash the cash.

This had been the extent of Shakira's personal experience with Reggie and his dodgy dealings. At least that had been the case until Reggie's missus Sam started bending the desk sergeant's ear on the blower, concerned that her fly-by-night husband had suddenly evaporated into the ether. Shakira was aware of the potential seriousness of this situation. She told Micky
"Sam would rather gnaw off her own foot than contact the enemy."
She persuaded Micky that,
"Her dilemma must have been an inkling that he had 'chanced his arm' once too often, with someone formidable, nothing trifling would have kept him away from his girls."
Micky, who was already aware of smatterings of Reggie's previous, agreed to give the situation a cursory glance. Interestingly the last child support payment traced back to some CCTV outside a bank in Eire. Reggie's encounter with Pint Pot, had been on his way to Ireland. He was endeavouring to avoid a formidable gang of Sikhs who he had poached from a London building company, before stumbling into another of his monetary setbacks. Unfortunately for him, this little firm got wind of his travels and 'settled their business' with him in South Dublin. At this point he was definitely still alive and kicking, or more accurately still alive after taking a kicking.
Shakira's background knowledge and a persuasive conversation with Julian had led Micky and Nick to the Holyhead ferry and Dublin, where they had tailed Reggie's tarnished reputation all the way to Foxford, County Mayo, where he eluded them by a whisker before fleeing the Emerald Isle for pastures new. Meanwhile, back at the factory, Shakira's paper trail of this bozo revealed a recent anomaly. Some of Reggie's previous creditors, had suddenly been paid off, indicating his physical presence in Norwich.

She quizzed Sam about it. All of her reticent and unhelpful response merely illustrated that she was an unconvincing liar. It did however reveal that any recovery of his finances was still insignificant and his feet were still embedded profoundly in the excrement. These circumstances made his prompt return to tax detectable, unlikely. Frustrated by Sam's silly fabrications' Shakira concluded she would extract more enlightenment by buying Pint Pot a drink in his local, The Farmhouse. Reggie's favourite bricklayer blabbed willingly,
"After he was seriously clobbered by the Sikhs and parted with a wad of folding money he went to ground. According to Dale and Jo he was on the missing list for a while. Not surprising really we all realised he was firmly in the fertiliser!"
Shakira's half interest in Pint Pot's slurred droning, abruptly became awakened when he mentioned Reggie's best friend.
"I suppose you knew Dale had a place in Portugal?" he asked, knowing full well that she didn't.
"Well Dale's wife's best friend Jo was supposed to join him"
This little dalliance was also hot news. "But they had a falling out and now she's working in Happisburg"
This conflab had been worth a couple of pints to Shakira who unearthed Jo's version from behind a bar in the seaside town, by the same method of extraction used on Pint-Pot.
Jo talked while sipping her free pint of lager in her short lunch break. She made it obvious any previous harmony with Reggie was dead in the water.
"Reggie was on his way out to Dale's place last time we spoke" she related sourly,
"I was supposed to go with him but I couldn't leave my daughter. One night we were both drunk and had an almighty row over it. I admit I can't remember much, but somehow I ended up with a shiner. Last I heard he was out there with some other woman."
When he returned from Eire, Shakira had related her findings to Micky, which included a Twitter account, bearing Dale's fizzog and name as well as Reggie's snaps of sunny Portugal.
"I've tried messaging him but to no avail and surprise, surprise the DWP have no current address"
"Even though I can smell another wild goose chase coming on Shakira" Micky grumbled,

"I suppose I am duty bound to find this numpty before he gets seriously hurt. Some bugger, somewhere, must be able to tell us who he's got wrong with, 'fore he get another ding!"

To this end, they reached the doorstep of Dale's holiday retreat where, as luck would have it he was neatly tucked up with a bottle of whiskey. Despite the unexpected arrival of a couple of British Boys in Blue he behaved with aplomb and without a smidgen of loyalty he insisted,

"Whatever Reggie has got hisself into, it's nothing to do with me. The last time he showed his ugly chops here was six months ago on his way back to Blighty. No one had seen hide nor hair of him since. He was supposed to bring Jo but they had a falling out"

"She hasn't seen him either" said Micky "Have you any idea why he is still under the radar Dale?"

"I have no clue, but if Sam has not heard from him it's not good, and by the way I'm not on Social Media"

Micky sent Shakira a text 'aborting his mission' and before anyone mentioned geese again, emailed Julian his request for a hasty retreat, with a suggestion that they might their detective skills might be better applied at The Brown Steed in Thetford, next to Reggie's last site. The next morning after she had dropped an apologetic note on Micky's desk, she snuck out before anything hit the fan and got to the pub before it opened. Diane and Liz had trawled through a plethora of stroppy drinkers all yesterday for a nugget to crack the stalemate and welcomed her assistance.

Micky, hot on Shakira's tail, arrived to overhear one 'happy chappy' telling her,

"I'm not surprised he's gone missing with some of the company he kept!"

"What company?" Micky interjected

"That Chris Robertson and his mates, not people I'd want to mess with," said the man.

Suddenly things began to make sense to Shakira who whispered,

"Sounds like Reggie's got himself tied up in something a bit naughtier than a bit of cash in hand. No wonder he's done another vanishing act."

As usual Shakira was able to expound accurately on this particular miscreant's misdemeanours, without the aid of the ACRO computer,
"This firm's usual merchandise is funny money." She expounded knowingly:
"Daddy dearest was nicked in the sixties for printing his own, and Chris was recently detained for similar, just when a new batch happened to hit the area. Reggie's dalliance with this branch of Thetford thuggery, might not just get him nicked for passing off a bit of monopoly money. That may have been the least of his worries, because any little messes down to his ineptitude, could have got callous Chris a long spell indoors, and this would easily have resulted in hazardous consequences for Reggie"

After checking the validity of Shakira's grapevine gossip and establishing that her assertions were irritatingly correct, Arthur called them back to an urgent meeting, in which he addressed the team,
"Shakira's right about Reggie. His downward spiral into unknown territory may well have got him in over his head. The realisation that this incompetent fool was a liability may have forced the hand of his callous employers. A judge has agreed to a search warrant for all the Robertson's shady enterprises"
He could see he was preaching to the converted all except Shakira,
"I wasn't saying the Robertson clan would have done away with him" she said," but they might just give him a nasty warning. We are talking about a semi-literate bloke here, with the IT skills of an educated chimp. Reggie has skid marks on his brow where things keep going over his head. I don't think they would have entrusted him with anything more complicated than passing off a few iffy notes. Personally I wouldn't send him out for a pack of fags" she protested
But Arthur had already run away with the idea that Reggie was in mortal danger,

"We have to remember that The Fraud Squad and the NCA are running the operation and it is therefore imperative that we take our lead from them." He raised his voice slightly in a bid to curtail the general contradictory rumbling,
"They have intelligence of a London gang operating in Thetford and concur that Chris and his dad fit like a glove. We know Reggie was pot-less until he bumped into Robertson in a local hostelry so our part of the bargain is to find this twit before he gets hurt. Err, Shakira I need to see you afterwards, you've been hacked again".
The way he neatly tacked this remark on the end bothered her, it was as if she was the entire reason they were playing second fiddle to other teams.
Meanwhile Julian instructed Diane to have another crack at Sam,
"She had indicated that she and the kids were out of the picture by the time his brickies got the work in Thetford, insisting she took no part in his business but I think she has always played the innocent. She may be a bit daft but she is smart enough to be entirely mercenary. After all she only contacted 'the filth' out of blind panic before some of his debts were settled. She may have been looking after her own interests. A touch more pressure, I think we might have squeezed out something vital."
"Tread you carefully, my woman" Micky added" if the dosh came from Chris & his Daddy's little printing scam, make sure we get the interviews sanctioned first, especially since they appear to have escalated into an international 3D cyber-crime"
Micky, thinking aloud said "Chris or one of his gorillas could have decided they wanted him out of the picture. He's already had one lamming and this lot were the more tooled up brand of bonkers"
"In that case, Julian" Liz urged "can I go back and badger some more of the charmers at The Brown Steed?"
"Actually, we've overstayed our welcome there" responded Micky "Chris is still in custody and his henchmen have been barred from most pubs in Thetford. Let's try that Spoons type pub nearest to Reggie's flat."
"I'm always in favour of a bit of old fashioned face to face." Julian chipped in.

The Farmfare manager was more helpful,
"I barred Reggie for sticking me with some dud notes and to be honest I was glad of the excuse to get shot of him and his mates. I'm only on relief so I can tell you anything you like as we are moving on next week."
"Alright then" asked Diane cheekily, "Where do you think they print the stuff?"
"Somewhere in the Brixton area apparently, but they know it's being watched and I should imagine the daft article would be lost in London whatever squit he talks about gangsters." He replied.
His mate chipped in,
"Didn't he get slung out of that old place up the road, trying to flog charlie."
Liz had heard a similar story before.
The manager whispered,
"I remembered a while back my mate Eric, barred him for selling some white powder. When he turned up here the other day I recognised him straight away, although he was a bit of a state. When I slung him out, he bragged to old Joe he'd get a late one off Eric on his way home. He'd have been clever, his pub's been shut for six months."
As they came out Diane met up with them,
"Sam is still giving me the run around." She seethed,
Shakira reaction was more cerebral,
"You know we are right near his old flat and we only have Sam's word for it that it's been sold"
The next day Shakira spoke to the estate agent on the phone, their Wymondham branch confirmed one of the flats clearly belonged to a Mrs Samantha Adams who had recently changed her mind about selling. They insisted it was empty but that there was probably still a key under the mat. When Micky and Liz got there late afternoon and knocked, no one answered, so they picked up the key from under the mat. Before they could unlock the door a neighbour approached them.
"Can I help at all?" she asked, seeing Liz in uniform,
"Yes please" said Micky flashing his warrant card "Does a Mrs Samantha Adams live here?"

"Oh no, not for a long time" said the neighbour "just her ex-husband Reggie. We are rarely graced with his presence these days, but he brought someone back here yesterday."
"Man or woman?" said Liz
"Sounded like a chap, they were having a right old go outside my door last night about twelve, one of them was definitely him" she reported scathingly "after the row the chap left.
Micky thanked her. He waited until she'd gone before he recovered the key and quietly gained entry. Before Liz could follow him in, he flew out, yelling for an ambulance. Reggie was slumped on the floor front room, a nasty blue colour with a very faint pulse. Despite their best efforts and prompt medical attention, he died of a cocaine overdose before they got him to hospital. There was even some left on a bricklayer's trowel beside him.

Chapter 10 Why Rocky?

Reggie's departure from this world had been regarded as a strange phenomenon. Perhaps the Robertsons were culpable, but if so proof was still many hours of hard graft away. Shakira had already put in long hours that day, just collating everything they had learned, so that the NCA could make a legally binding verification of the facts. Always the main body of police work was the proof. An essential element, way before any presentation to a court.

Exhausted she had fallen asleep on the sofa in front of the telly waiting for Rocky to come back from work. When she woke up, she experienced that weird sensation that happens when you're not sure what time of day it is. When fully conscious she had become certain that it was after eleven at night so she searched the annals of her memory for a date on Rocky's calendar. Surely he should have been home hours ago. She tried his mobile, which irritatingly went to voicemail. She checked on the kids and then rang again to no avail. She had convinced herself he could look after himself, and that he would turn up in a taxi at some unearthly hour, probably a little worse for wear. Still shattered she went to bed.

About five o'clock she was shaken out of her slumber by her kids asking where Dad was. She tried to communicate a vague pretence of knowing his whereabouts, while really thinking, "Where the bleeding hell was Dad? I bet the silly bugger thinks he has told me about some works beano or something"

As time went on she started to worry big time, as he would not have forgotten she had to work this morning. She rang his mobile, still nothing. "Daddy must be spark out on someone's floor." She thought. Having determined it was time to ring work she stood looking at her handset trying to decide whose number to dial. As if by magic it rang and it was Micky.

"It's OK!" he responded at once before she could speak, "Rocky is here!"

"What the fuck was he doing there?" Upset and angry, she swore at her boss for the first time, although her expletive was clearly directed at Rocky, "He should have been here hours ago, getting the kids ready for school!" she spluttered assuming he had gone to report some minor traffic incident.
"And where hell has he been all night? I'm sorry Micky, can you put him on the phone please?"
"You don't understand Shakira he is helping us with our enquiries!" he stuttered vaguely.
"What enquiries?" she blustered, taking the phrase literally still assuming it was Rocky's fault.
"He is being interviewed!" he said diplomatically.
"You are not making sense Micky, about what?" she thundered, finally pointing the blame at Micky.
"Look" he said with just a little more aplomb "he is corroborating evidence" and even less lucidly "They may have to arrest him but I can't tell you any more than that at the moment!"
"I'll be right there!" she yelled angrily slamming down the phone and immediately picking it up again.
"Hello Mariska I'm sorry I need a favour, are you working today? No I hoped you weren't. Can you have the kids, Rocky's at the police station" she blurted illogically still trying to sound calm.
"I'll be right round!" her neighbour replied compliantly, sensing her panic. She arrived quick as a flash, soon after Shakira put the phone down. Mariska began carting her four charges off to school in sensible silence trying to mask her curiosity, assuming an explanation would ensue later.
On her way to retrieve Rocky on the bus, because for some reason he seemed to have the vehicle, the awful truth started dawning on Shakira and her mind started racing. She wondered what they had found out about her, perhaps she had not been as clever about things as she thought. This interrogation could not possibly have been about Rocky.

She had this uncomfortable feeling that they had uncovered the piece of Shakira she had hoped to keep under wraps, the one that could have lead her into a huge minefield of big, bad trouble. She had long been aware that being the person she was and working with the police, left her sailing close to the wind. She assumed whatever they were ostensibly quizzing Rocky about was because she had not covered her tracks properly.

Suddenly, paranoia had got its teeth into her and would not let go. Wild phobia's raced around her head uncontrollably. Local rumours that they were both gangsters and some of Rocky's wind ups hadn't helped, but none of them knew the real Shakira. Even when he'd had a few Rocky was pretty guarded about what he let slip. Surely they could not know everything.

What if they caught up with her and sent her to prison. How would she cope? Would they conclude Rocky was an 'Accessory After the Fact.' Curtailing her more her wild thoughts and pretending some sort of normality she tried to enter her place of work. The desk sergeant stopped her in her tracks.

"I've been told to ask you not to use your fob, please follow me," he recited his instructions coldly as if they were strangers, "Please wait in here Ms Browning.DS Saint will be along to see you shortly!"

She could not think properly under this kind of pressure. She tried desperately to concentrate on what they could possibly have discovered.

'Corroborating evidence' the words had been doing handstands round her brain ever since they were spoken. Perhaps in deciding Rocky was her Achilles heel they were using him to make her confess. They knew how she felt about Rocky. She had made it obvious to them that she would admit to everything to keep him out of it.

She waited interminably and wished Micky would at least get on with it and put her out of her misery. She started to recall her visits to imprisoned women and the survival strategy the girls were told to think about. A nurse in the segregation unit sarcastically described HMP Holloway as "A government scheme designed to prevent the clogging-up of the overcrowded mental health provision and to stop the authorities dealing with messy suicides."

Would she survive incarceration? What if they arrested both of them? What would become of her children? She would have to launch an appeal from inside to get him freed. Would he ever forgive her?

Eventually Micky arrived and plonked himself down opposite her just as she was bordering on hysteria.

"I'll be as candid as I can" he opened with a severe expression which did nothing to calm her fears,

"There has been some unexplained gaps in many of our ongoing investigations. The only connecting factor seemed to be your husband, so we need to extract every piece of relevant information in order to clear him!" He rambled not very candidly.

She began cautiously and strategically taking a deep breath, "Clear him of what? Are you suggesting Rocky is guilty of some offence. What exactly is he being accused of?"

"I can't say at the moment." he said after a long silence!

"Right Micky!" she said decisively "On which criminal's say so are you suggesting Rocky is involved in something illegal? Or is this just a strategy the force use to make people confess to something they haven't done?"

Another tacit reply, although she probably deserved this bout of silence.

"You must be able to tell me what you are charging him with" she demanded, hedging her bets.

Still no answer. So she screamed frantically,

"If you thought I would just sit here without explanation and just roll over to keep my job you must be deluded. And don't think I won't go to the Chief Constable, whoever that is." Then she blurted out even more bravely.

"If you want to get rid of me, sack me but don't try and bully my family!"

"OK Shakira I'll level with you" he said calmly "we thought it was coincidence at first, but in almost every case you have worked on there has been anomalies and in some cases unexplained deaths so we need to investigate."
"So ……WHY ROCKY?" she yelled exasperatedly and beside herself, not to mention giving too much away.
"Because in all these mysteries his name is the only connection"
"WHICH CASES?" she yelled again.
"ALL OF THEM" Micky yelled louder.
She had never heard Micky yell like that before. It had made her step back to take stock of the situation. She realised she was on thin ice if she questioned his reasoning too much. They were both silent for a moment and then he said, after regaining his own composure.
"Right then I will try and make sense of it all if you'll just listen for a change!" he conceded,
"Firstly there was this thing with Jonathan!" he said quietly
"Don't get me started on that twat" she lashed out, losing the plot again, but relieved to be diverting the attention "What's that tosser accused Rocky of now? He wouldn't know the truth if it ran him over"
"He was beaten up by someone who told him he was Rocky's best friend!" he said.
"Rubbish!" she said more quietly "He is an inveterate liar and none of Rocky's friends are given to random acts of violence. I expect someone lumped him one for stirring the shit for them the way he's done with me and Rocky!"
Micky apparent belief of this flagrant falsehood irked her even more. Whatever happened to her she did not want Rocky to be a scapegoat for something she'd done wrong and she was not having this.
Still vaguely imagining Rocky going to end up in prison on her behalf she regained her ability to think on her feet and discerned that the solution to Rocky's exculpation, in this instance, must lay in the real story.
"Before you start spouting more of Johnathan's porkies, you listen to me for a moment Micky. Jonathan and Rocky had been acquainted for some time, because the delinquent daughter went to school with our kids.

"Rocky tolerated her in the house, because no one else ever seemed to be minding her. When Jonathan said he was desperate for work Rocky got him a job at the same factory. Suddenly Rocky found he was being bullied for no reason other than some apparent fabrication by Jonathan to ingratiate himself with a manager. Then he got Rocky sent to Coventry by the others, that's the way Jonathan works.

"Rocky just flipped jobs before any real harm ensued, then Jonathan's nasty little scheme back-fired on him. After Rocky left, they sacked this manager and got rid of useless Jonathan for good measure, so his sycophantic hypocrisy didn't work there, although you lot seem to be impressed by it here.

"Then for good measure the toffee nosed little shithead started messing with me at the housing office. I'm less tolerant than my husband and as I was the numpty's senior they just moved him on. Then I had the misfortune to encounter his stupid games here, he's like a wasp you can't shake him off without getting stung.

"Unfortunately, people leaving prison expect less than most of us and tend to put up with his incompetent drivel. If anyone did actually hurt him physically I expect he well deserved it, but it certainly wasn't anything to do with Rocky."

"There was a witness" said Micky

"I doubt it" she continued confidently, although a little confused "what kind of witness?"

Whatever Micky was playing at, she had been convinced this tall tale was the invention of a Jonathan imaginary friend,

"The Pub Manager" said Micky with conviction "He swears his intervention was the only thing that stopped Rocky's mate beating Jonathan to death. Julian took a statement from him"

This stunned Shakira into silence, she knew Micky was clever, but this was a strange tactic to extract some sort of confession from her. This complete fabrication was all over the place and very unlike Micky. Maybe someone fooled Julian into the idea that Rocky was party to this fairy-tale, and even then they must have been convincing.

If Jonathan had any real ammunition he could use detrimentally about either of them, he would have done so by now. She may have been a little naïve about how much she could keep from Micky and Julian but the entire police force had taken her for a fool from the get go, so it was unlikely they knew the half of it. Whatever Micky had uncovered, spouting this red-herring of hearsay was as uncharacteristic as it was unprofessional. As if reading her mind Micky changed tack,
"Forget Jonathan a mo. I want to know why you took Rocky to Nottingham?" he asked. She thought carefully and replied with verity,
"You know why, for the reasons *you* gave me the permission." Micky had never denied this fact, so she attempted to enlarge on her answer truthfully,
"He had an in depth knowledge and experience of the place and anyway I was not sure I could trust my colleagues to be there for me if anything went wrong. I thought I could use our contacts there to find the china white dealer operating in Norwich which, to be fair, I did"
She paused to consider carefully. It occurred to her that some piece of scum from Nottingham could have fed Micky a load of cobblers, perhaps she'd better shut-up now and find out the facts first. Micky interrupted her thoughts,
"Look Shakira, I promise I will explain everything when they have finished interviewing Rocky. I need to send you home now, I'll ring you as soon as I have something to tell you."
Micky's brutal brush off upset her more than any of the rest of it and the tears came without warning,
"It's a conspiracy" she sobbed still trying to think on her feet
"What could you possibly think Rocky has done wrong that could justify threatening to arrest him? Are you fitting up Rocky just because he knows a few criminals in Norwich and Nottingham?
"You should have realised by now Jonathan is a nasty gossip who uses people by telling barefaced lies, that does not mean Rocky would hurt the idiot, he's more grown up than that. You've been dealing with nasty people for too long Micky, you think everyone is a criminal"

Desperately groping for the moral high-ground, her fury over-rode her common sense, not to mention her desire to know if any of her own secrets were behind this apparent accusation. She thought better than to continue and extricated herself before she said something stupid and got herself in any deeper. She headed towards the door weeping in floods.
"Wait Shakira, I'll get someone to take you back in an unmarked car!" he called after her.
"I wouldn't bother on my account, all my neighbours already know my business. Rocky's detention is probably in the local paper by now". As she stormed out slamming the door. Liz ran after her,
"Whatever's happened?" she said innocently,
"Just leave me alone. Don't try and pretend you are not part of this crap as well, because you are just as two faced as the rest of the bastards!" Shakira replied with venom "Go and patronise someone else!"
As she tried to remove herself quickly, a DS she did not know, stopped her dead and ordered her to follow them. Now she was really worried. Was this the end of her career and her freedom? She was trying to work out where she had slipped-up. He just opened the car door placidly for her and drove her back home in silence. She tried to get out, but of course police cars are internally locked. Turning to her captor she waited insolently expecting to be read her rights.
"I'm sorry Ms Browning, I've got to take all your Police ID and cards off you until they have finished with your husband!"
Much as this was not a good sign, it was not as bad as she had feared. He let her out and she ran to the front door sobbing, hoping this temporary freedom would give her breathing space. After some consideration she decided the best course of action was just to sit it out, until she was enlightened or Rocky returned.
She had calmed down by the time Mariska returned with the kids and Shakira thanked her, assuring her everything was fine, but she did ask her to keep it quiet and she dumbed down the drama by saying Rocky was just helping the police with some of her work.

Insecure as she was, she trusted Rocky not to drop her in it. Whatever they knew about either of them, he was easily smart enough to convince them the whole thing was ridiculous and they had made a big mistake. They had held him for much more than 24 hours by now, anyway. She was still running through a gamut of emotions most of which was guilt. Had she put her husband's whole future at risk for a job or had it been something she had done?

Eventually, and with considerable bravery she rang Micky to demand Rocky should have a solicitor.

"Look, Shakira I told you it would all be OK" he prattled as if nothing had happened "He has not been charged and is here of his own volition. He will be back home as soon as they have all the information they need" Shakira slammed the phone down.

It wasn't until about six the next morning Rocky returned. She saw them pull up, it was the same plain clothes DS and unmarked car. Rocky seemed remarkably unscathed, considering his ordeal, regarding the whole thing as a tremendous adventure, so ludicrous that he could only be amused by their stupidity.

Certain that there would be no peace otherwise, he began his narration of events which had proved to be much more bizarre than Shakira could have possibly imagined. Hearing the way he had been treated, you would not only think her gentle husband a potential felon, but was somehow guilty of abetting wholesale slaughter across the length and breadth of the country.

"Julian took me to a room with two blokes I didn't know." he had begun,

"In addition to accusing me of orchestrating some kind of assault on dopey Jonathan, as if anyone need bother, he seemed to imply I was in cahoots with this numbskull Darius. I patiently tried to explain that although I had heard the name in connection to a case, I did not actually know the man. Then they showed me an old photo of what looked like some schoolkid, I said truthfully he was vaguely familiar, but I did not have a penchant for little boys if that was the charge. They were not amused. Then they showed me a more recent mugshot. I told them I had definitely seen him somewhere, but I could not recall where from.

"Next they came to Ethan. I was expecting this so I fessed up to going over there to smoke a bit of weed with him and a couple of other mates, long before he got nicked or you worked with the law".

"Oh for god's sake Rocky" she blurted out,

"I did make it quite clear you would have gone bonkers if you had known, not only because it was illegal but more importantly because you were left minding the kids while I was out smoking puff. I told them I was much more scared of incurring your wrath than theirs. Despite the threat of arrest it was hard to take them seriously.

"The odd thing was, they were singularly uninterested in Ethan or his dope and only wanted to know if Jack was there with us." Seeking confirmation she asked, "You've never met Jack have you?"

"Well that was where it went really weird. Out of the blue one of them accused me of wanting to get rid of Jack. I insisted there was no logic in their speculation as I had never met the man and only knew what Leila had said about him"

He carried on regardless asking, "We were told Nikos had a contract out on him."

"I told them to have a word with themselves, if they thought I was involved in a contract. Not only had I never set eyes on Jack, but all I knew about Nikos is that he had some questionable friends from Essex.

"I went on to say, I don't want to blame the missus who is much more ferocious than you two, but Leila was an old pal of hers who I'd only met a few times. I explained it was fortunate for Jack that he had never encountered Shakira, because she wouldn't need a contract to scare him to death. More to the point I added, as far as I last heard Jack is still alive and well and causing havoc somewhere miles away from here, I hope"

"So when they finally let me go they told me you were there waiting for me, I held up my wrists for the cuffs and demanded they put me in a cell. They laughed."

Rocky was enjoying the excitement but Shakira was understandably terrified by it all. Undeterred by her glum expression he pressed on,

"At one point they mentioned Hal. I explained what happened in The Shark's Tooth. I admitted reading him the riot act but they were unconcerned about that too. They asked if I knew anyone else in the pub I said I didn't remember recognising anyone but I had had a few and it was dark."

"When they started trying to point the finger about Byrnsey as if I'd had him knocked off in some fit of jealousy. I laughed and said that it was clearly complete bollocks, that you had known him way before I met you and I had barely even known Eddie Alba who you had worked for briefly in some pub.

"They wanted to know if Emmanuel Byrne had tried to sell our new address to the estate thugs. I side-stepped this by explaining when we left London Eddie was the one of the few people who actually knew we were in Norwich. Only the police had our actual address. I told them that their tenuous connection was preposterous and that I wanted my prints and DNA taken off the system, as they obtained them under false pretences. I had only submitted them because I thought it was helping your work, but now they seemed to be trying to fit me up I did not want to be so generous with my personal data."

"What the hell did you say that for?" interrupted Shakira unable to stop herself from yelling at him.

"Because, my darling, they were trying to intimate you or I were involved with some violent gang," he yelled back defensively, "I mean do you want me to tell you what happened?" he said wearily "you don't want me miss out an important detail, do you?"

She apologised "I'm sorry I'm just very tired, I thought they were just testing my loyalty when they asked for your DNA, but later Nick said they thought you might have been in Sid's studio, but as I knew you hadn't, I put it out of my mind and forgot all about it. It didn't seem worth talking about at the time"

"They also asked me about Alan," he continued,

"When they carried on as if I had done away with this Blake on his behalf, I sarcastically pointed out we only stood next to each other sorting post. Not planning a gang heist and that I was Alan's union rep not his criminal accomplice. Anyway I had never even seen this Blake bloke who I understood he fell in the river pissed while you lot were chasing him. At the particular time Alan and I were getting earache off the new sheriff."
Shakira also started to mull over the recent spate of fatalities. By London standards the number would have been unfortunate but not unexceptional, but for Norwich almost a little backwater in comparison. Even she was coming round to the idea some other factor was at work here.
Rocky interrupted her train of thought by asking if she was listening. She had to admit she had drifted off. She tried desperately not to look pensive, but he seemed oblivious. He was too busy being amused by it all, coppers had accused him of made up nonsense before and he was not impressed, but he had thought Shakira knew Micky better.
Rocky went on to recount their next issue
"Then they asked why I disliked Frazer, I said I disliked a lot of racists and irritating as his attempts to goad me into combat were, I found him easy to ignore. So they said how fortuitous it was that my wife had discovered the murder weapon, despite a whole constabulary missing it. I afraid this led me to imply that this was because they were a stupid bunch of bumpkins and you were not."
She interjected "Perhaps they had come to the soppy conclusion you were the northerner he was drinking with, forgetting we would have been easily recognised and only stopped frequenting the place because of him"
Shakira knew intimating that she had planted the bat was silly- especially as Micky hardly left her side while they had re-enacted Frazer's possible steps.

"Then they said I had battered Reggie, because he owed me money" he yawned "I made it quite clear that as I was not trusted with a bank account and only got pocket money if I had been good, so my investing money in a dodgy builder without your permission would have been out of the question. As for turning up with Pint Pot to get his wages there was never an occasion for fisticuffs. He weighed him in without question and bought us a pint each to shut us up.

Shakira's training had told her that this ran like the orchestration of a proper interrogation and it was likely they had checked Rocky's alibis for each occasion. There was something going on at the nick that neither she nor Rocky were party to. Surely they must have worked out by now that the henchman that they imagined went round Norwich sorting people out on Rocky's behalf were figments of someone's imagination.

Although Shakira's extraction of information had been much more torturous than theirs Rocky suddenly remembered a message from Micky, telling her to take today off as well and he would see her tomorrow. Grateful even for that half-arsed piece of communication from her boss, Shakira tried to mull things over calmly while Rocky slept. It was apparent to her that she was often her own worst enemy. Going to meet a known copper's nark in London with criminal connections without telling anyone was a bit rash but why had they treated Rocky to this stupid ordeal? She had found the situation increasingly disturbing as Rocky's tale had unfolded. Dumfounded by his revelations Shakira was suddenly hearing those alarm bells again. Could her recent history really throw up so many coincidences, or was someone stalking her by computer? More to the point…. Why Rocky?

Chapter 11 The End of the Road, or is it?

As a result of his enforced stay in Wymondham's worst hotel, a short altercation ensued on Rocky's return to work. Nevertheless, he emerged reasonably unscathed having successfully cited 'Official Union Business' as the cause of his absence.

After his first shift, he arrived home to find Shakira snoring on the sofa and the kids running riot. Once he had put them to bed, he chilled out by having a quiet look at Facebook while she slept.

Of late Shakira's Facebook page had thrown out weird messages. Some religious nut had put 'the end is nigh' on her timeline. He had meant to mention it to her, but he did not want to interfere with her choice of friends. He satisfied himself that if she had any concerns she would have been prompted her to get some IT wizard on the case.

At six in the morning, he and Shakira had been woken up by the almost predictable knock on the door. The two plain clothed officers standing in her hallway demanded she attend the station. Before she could protest one reeled off her rights, while the other handed her a warrant and went through her pockets, although they did not search the house. As they left, Rocky went through the gamut of emotions from anger to the feeling of emasculation borne out of being totally helpless against the power of the law, despite his shock at their stupidity.

He had registered Shakira's look of inevitability as she was shoved into the unmarked car. For the first time through his anger and incredulity, he mused over the fact that even a judge must have been convinced by this ridiculous load of old tripe. He had laughed off the accusations during *his* ordeal, but for Shakira it was serious. Even the possibility that there was something she had not told him, flashed through his mind until he realised this nonsense was making him paranoid.

Questioning whether Shakira's interminable fight for justice had been worth all the drama, he started to blame himself for not seeing this coming and his inherent mistrust of the police began to kick in. At this point his common sense prevailed and two things dawned on him. The first was that the kids were not up for school yet, the second was so obvious he shouted it out loud,

"Shit! She needs a solicitor!"

Back at 'the shop' they had kept Shakira waiting for a couple of hours so she was almost tearing her hair out. She wiped her tears and began trying to compose herself as a DS she vaguely recognised entered the room quietly, and almost mysteriously. His salt and pepper hair was in a sort of quiff and he was dressed like an ice cream. Yellow polo shirt, powder blue trousers and a pink tie. His attire put her in mind of a Cowardesque butler, who when asked to describe his master's new suit, tactfully replied, "A trifle sudden for my liking sir!"

As they sat in silence an unfamiliar man joined him. He was much taller and chunkier than the first. Instead of the hard man image he obviously intended, his black hair, dark suit, white shirt and black tie made him look more like an undertaker.

The second one said politely "I'm sorry to have kept you waiting" and muttered some sort of introduction. Shakira was not listening. Her mind was still turning somersaults and disjointedly re-living recent events. The institution she had always trusted implicitly, had suddenly become her enemy. Those prison gates slipped back in her mind's eye and before she could staunch them and more outrageous thoughts zipped round her head, without her body catching up. Trying to focus was impossible.

Mister Ice-cream started by asking "You are obviously conversant with what the law means by 'Perverting the course of Justice' and 'Perjury'." His matter-of-factness made it sound like a review of her coursework rather than an accusation. On discernment of this pretence of friendly chit-chat, she felt herself losing the plot, so she kept quiet. Although she was dying to speak she decided her tacit defiance had better suffice at this juncture. He looked slightly uncomfortable and fell silent.

It occurred to her that he was no poker player. He made it obvious he had rehearsed replies to any objections and wondered why this outspoken woman was not fighting back.

After a pregnant pause her outrage got the better of her,

"Well I have a 2/1 Criminology degree with honours, how conversant do you think I am?"

No one spoke again and eventually she cracked,

"Look I'm finding this whole experience very harrowing, you haven't even assigned me a solicitor, an essential part of the law you are so keen to test me on. It would also be helpful if you had indicated which course of justice you think I've perverted"

"Just answer the questions!" the ice cream one demanded obviously slightly rankled.

"Remind me of your names again?" she said as if to put him in his place "I did not catch them!"

"DS Keith Gilbert and this is DS James Jericco" he said indicating accordingly "We introduced ourselves when we came in!"

"I was not really paying attention I was still upset at being dragged here by officers from my own workplace!"

Jericco, the undertaker, quickly changed the subject.

"Your husband seems to know a lot of people in Norwich, Shakira!" he said,

She did not reply, so he continued "Were you aware he was friendly with so many criminals?"

"Naturally I know most of the people my husband does," she snapped "but we are not joined at the hip. I've never felt the need to request that he interrogates everyone he has a pint with, to give them an opportunity to confess any past misdemeanours, before they sip their beer." Reprovingly she added

"Then again *I* believe in giving people the benefit of the doubt "

Aware she was losing it again, she pulled back and continued slowly with a passive smile,

"You must have met a fair few criminals yourself, but hopefully, like Rocky and I, you are an advocate of rehabilitating offenders. It is my understanding that senior police officers are expected to be non-judgemental."

"You are not out of the woods yet, my young lady!" Jericco bristled, not quite picking up her inference.

"Was that some kind of threat or have you resorted to patronising me? I am neither titled nor your young anything. I have not, so far been given the privilege of knowing what 'woods' I am trying to get out of.

"First you held my husband without proper charges, with spurious attempts at some groundless accusation. Now you have trumped up this charge on the basis that I tampered with evidence. WHAT EVIDENCE?"

She had resolved to maintain her defensive stance until she pushed them into some sort of proper exposition.

"OK Shakira, did you remove something from the lab?" Gilbert blurted out angrily almost in spite of himself.

"From Becky's lab? You must be joking, the imputation is preposterous! Surely, even off the top of your head you could manage a better story than that. Becky would never have let an item of evidence out of her sight, let alone out of her little empire. It's a blatant fabrication not worthy of a detective" she replied coolly "In fact it is such a daft allegation I won't even dignify it with a response. Let's be honest since the get go, none of my line managers have had the good grace to put any trust in me to do my job, let alone allowed me an opportunity to mess with forensics.

After a short hiatus she went on,

"If so much as an eyelash had been missing within a mile of anywhere I had been, you would have checked the CCTV there and then. It must be painfully clear that I would not know where to look for something in the lab, let alone remove it without being caught 'en flagrante!' If you really intend prosecuting me, you will have to invent something more credible than that."

Gilbert who appeared to be asking the more direct questions, tried another tack,

"Why did you go to Soho on your own Shakira?"

"At last a vaguely relevant question, even if you do already have a documented answer." she criticised. "I knew the place well and hoped my ground-level knowledge would uncover the dealer we were looking for!"

Gilbert went on "So you are insisting you did not know Darius before you spoke to Don in London, even though Rocky did!"

Shakira took a deep breath,

"Rocky did not know Darius either. He has always had a photographic memory for faces, even if he does not know the person, it's a part of his talent for art. He could have easily bumped into the bloke when he lived in Nottingham. I didn't discuss my reasons for going to London with Rocky either. I had wanted to see how it panned out. Until uncovering a definite connection at the Dog and Trumpet, I had not been certain my guesswork was correct. In fact it was only when Darius walked into The Dog to meet Micky, that I recognised him from his mugshot. If I'd ever clapped eyes on him before that I don't remember and Rocky's was a hazy recollection of his face. I don't suppose he'd ever been an art student, the geezer?"

They interrogated her for about two hours then an urgent message called them away swiftly. Jericco returned briefly and handed her a sandwich and a cup of coffee. As he left she asked him if Rocky was still with the kids and he assured her he was. She was left with just one PC at the door for about an hour.

On their return they seemed to behave quite differently. Shakira thought perhaps they had been warned there would be repercussions if they bullied wrongfully arrested colleagues, even if their remit was to put them in the dock.

Gilbert fumbled in his briefcase and showed her a photo on his tablet that had been taken in The Eagle and asked politely.

"Please can you tell me who this is?"

"That's Kenny!" she said surprised by this apparent diversion" Kenny McCann. I haven't seen him for years, what the hell has he got to do with the price of fish?"

Irritated by this apparent irrelevance she wondered if he had photos of all the Eagle's bar-flies.

"You do know him then?" he persisted

"Of course I know him", she said thoughtfully, still wondering why he was being discussed,

"As I'm sure you are aware, I went out with him years ago in London and then later we just shared a flat. Then about twenty years ago he left London and went to live back in Nottingham when he met Rocky! If you are going to quiz me about all my old boyfriends we could be here a long time. "

"When did you last see him?" he continued, ignoring her sarcasm.

"About five years ago in The Eagle. He was one of many mutual friends Rocky and I had but this was the first time he'd seen us together. In fact one of the reasons we had popped in was to surprise him Kenny again, but when we arrived we discovered Kenny had gone to The States. Anyway Darius never goes in The Eagle apparently"

Jericco chipped in,

"Who told you that? Bernie, or people in the pub?"

Shakira nodded and "Mmmed!" an agreement and then said "Both I think"

"Which part of America had he gone to?" Jericco went on,

"Oh Kenny, err they didn't say but I naturally assumed it must be Oregon, lots of my muso mates moved out there."

Before they asked anything else she burst in aggressively,

"Despite your change of tone you are still not being very perspicuous. What particular aspect of my relationship with Kenny are you *so* excited by?"

The last bit was so flirtatious it made them noticeably uncomfortable, then her mind wandered back to Darius.

"Oh wait a minute, Kenny would have had nothing to do with smack if that's where you are going. If he did know Darius, I doubt he would have much to do with him."

"How did you and Rocky meet Kenny" Gilbert persisted, revealing a disinterest in Darius again.

Shakira was still curious as to why he was more interested in a very ex-boyfriend, than a smack dealer who had killed himself before a possible murder charge, but she responded calmly as she wanted to follow his train of thought.

"Well as I explained, Rocky and I met Kenny at different times in different cities. I met Kenny when he was playing in my mate's band in London. We went out for a short time, drifted apart and as I said, ended up as flatmates. Way after that Rocky did an art degree in Nottingham. Kenny happened to be his best mate there, until they fell out."

His next question threw her completely.

"Why did they fall out, was Kenny jealous?"

"Sorry, you are not paying attention" she muttered crisply "This was way before I met Rocky and anyway Kenny was not the jealous type! Our relationship was not like that"

In truth it had never really occurred to her. She tried to clarify,

"Monogamy wasn't very fashionable then. If Kenny was obsessive, it was about music and booze, not particular women."

After some consideration, but without any concept of the direction in which the conversation was supposed to be heading she said,

"Has something happened to Kenny?"

"Not as far as we know!" Jericco wittered.

"Being so nearby you must have seen him when he was staying in Norwich." Gilbert asked oddly

After some thought about this strange tactic she said,

"You've got yourselves confused somewhere. He may have done the odd gig here, but he only found out Rocky and I knew each other when we saw him in the Eagle. He didn't even ask where we lived, and that was about five years ago!" She said as if it was obvious.

"You did not go to his flat in Thorpe St Andrew then?" he said dubiously.

"Who Kenny? Nah! You've definitely got your wires crossed. That's where we live. Kenny never lived in Norwich, he doesn't even like the place. What a strange thing to say, whatever makes you think he'd live here?"

She paused for a minute and then said. "Is Kenny OK?"

Although less aggressive, this irrelevant and bizarre line of questioning was making her really insecure. She thought maybe that was their intention.

"Look, I have no idea what game you are playing but I'm entitled to a solicitor. I have not seen Kenny for about five years and if we are talking about Darius I don't even know the man. I would like to go home now!"

They looked at each other and nodded in agreement! One of them turned off the digital recording.

Then Jericco said quietly,

"We apologise for putting you through this, but you two are your own worst enemies Shakira. While you were busy being cagey because of some ancient and minor misdemeanours, we nearly missed discovering the truth. Your reluctance to clarify certain matters, made it difficult for us to clear you. Also you were so embroiled in the local community and all of your acquaintances seem to have criminal histories. You and Rocky appeared to be the only common denominator in some mysterious fatalities. Until we just got the positive ident on the DNA we thought was Rocky's, we could not rule out the pair of you"

He stopped for a moment and said "We are now pretty convinced you and Rocky are innocent despite knowing the person we are looking for!"

"Innocent? What did you think Rocky was guilty of and what about his DNA. What exactly are you investigating? Who is the person you are looking for? If it's not Darius who is it and why would they know Kenny?"

Attempting to field her questions Jericco insisted,

"We are not at liberty to say, but the results will be revealed presently"

Gilbert added unhelpfully "This is an on-going investigation and we are relying on your discretion Shakira."

As she was already tearful and feeling betrayed, his parting remark got right up her nose.

Julian came into the room first. "I am truly sorry we had to do this Shakira!" he said as she sobbed quietly.

"Surely you must have realised we looked into your slightly chequered past before you got here. It's true most people in Norfolk do not have such close connections with the City's scoundrels, but only a very few of your colleagues are completely unblemished you know. You appeared to be so embroiled in some of the infractions that you also appeared complicit. Being arrested at the odd demo, and smoking the odd spliff hardly makes you Kenneth Noye"

"I'm still not convinced you weren't trying to fit me up for not being one of your little clique of goody-goodies!" she grizzled quietly.

"Once, when you first came, I joked with Arthur that you must be a criminal to know all these ne'er do wells" Julian said "and you looked at me as if you had just robbed a bank!" she stopped sobbing and laughed as she remembered it so well! By this time Micky had come in the room and put his arm round her.

When Micky left the room briefly and then returned. Julian explained he had gone to ring Rocky to also put him out of his misery.

Julian tried to explain "You and Rocky were only suspected of involvement because you knew someone in so many open cases and then they lost that bloody DNA…."

"So there really was a theft from the lab then, but why the hell would you think it was me?" she interrupted

"Well actually no, there wasn't, but there were a lot of unexplained situations to clear up. When he said "unexplained" her mind started racing. Could he be talking about missing persons or could they be dealing with a murder? She was barely listening as he went on.

"This was new territory for me, it was only when we identified the DNA on the bat we realised…" he trailed off again,

"So if you have the DNA whose is it? Does it belong to Frazer's killer?"

"I will go through the finer points with you later Shakira" Micky interjected and then Julian concluded,

"Never in my life have I known two perfectly innocent people to have been so, well…" he trailed off

"SO CLOSE TO MURDER!" Micky yelled exasperated.

Chapter 12 Is this Justice?

Having almost fully composed herself, Shakira sipped coffee while Julian embarked uncomfortably on a transcript of the events she had previously not been a party to. She watched him struggle, with his usual difficulty which she described as 'Not engaging brain before opening mouth'. In order to avoid this, his narrative was laboured with deep breaths before each phrase,

"I'm sure you would agree that Becky is sceptical about anything, unless it is backed by science. When Anna found the Filofax, she had been adamant it was her first visit to Sid's personal space since the tragedy. She explained she had only ventured into this sepulchre and its reminders of darkness immediately after you left, because of your kind words, about bereavement and the healing process.

"Its discovery, prompted Becky to dispatch a new CSM to take a fresh look at Sid's chaotic legacy, still allegedly untouched.

"Becky decided to quiz you about the Filofax because it had materialised immediately after your first visit to Anna's. Coincidentally, but not serendipitously for you, the absence of the DNA sample, still unmatched from the original forensic sweep, came to light just as you had left the lab after your second visit with Micky.

"When The Crime Scene Analysts had tried to take a further specimen the substance had been eradicated. All that remained on the sofa was the same disinfectant with which the Filofax was cleaned. It was a domestic chemical never used on the farm and Anna had scoffed at the idea she had a sudden impulse to start spring cleaning.

"Admittedly, somewhat jumping to conclusions, and reasonably unacquainted with your haphazard methods, Becky toyed with the idea that the DNA might have belonged to Rocky. This was mainly based on Hal's insistence that he and Rocky were bosom pals before the incident in The Shark's Tooth. It seemed logical to her, that Rocky may have known Sid and visited the studio.

"Micky and I totally dismissed her inference that you had planted the Filofax, or indeed would have interfered with the analysis of anything in the lab. Under these circumstances and to show neutrality we thought it best to send Rocky's sample to Cambridge for comparison. As it was not a priority it took them three months."

"So whose was it? Who did it really belong to?" Shakira interrupted impatiently.

"I was getting to that bit" Julian said equally impatiently in his long-winded way. After a look from Micky he said,

"Perhaps Michael would explain it better".

Micky began purposefully, visibly thinking on his feet,

"Years ago, before there was a proper database, a man was arrested and his details were taken after a rum ol' barney in a pub. He had insisted he hadn't thrown any punches himself, but admitted instigating the fight by winding up some local thug. Initially he had clammed up pleading an alibi of absence, insisting at the time of the melee he was still propping up the pub's other bar. In which case the blood down his front begged a question. When quizzed about it, he removed his shirt stroppily, and threw it to the officer. Later he made a sultry admission that he had 'copped it' after all because tests proved all the blood was his and none belonged to the victim. He insisted he did not want the shirt back so obligingly it was bagged and retained."

"Then, after tracing the lab assistant responsible, the misplaced sample was recovered from the genomic freezer, but its owner's identity was still not located on the system. Later an efficient bod from Nottingham put the shirt's profile on the computer, and it was picked up here on a routine check. By the time it was accurately verified, you were with Gilbert and Jericco."

"So you admit we were both persecuted needlessly." said Shakira as her cogwheels worked overtime to recall recent events,

"Hang on a minute, Nottingham, You knew it wasn't Rocky's and had Darius on file….. Oh my god ….Kenny? Was it Kenny McCann?"

A silence ensued while Shakira visibly absorbed the repercussions of this possibility. Micky's account had almost skimmed across this logical conclusion,

"It was only recently that they had connected the studio contribution to Kenny's shirt." Julian blurted,

"Then Becky remembered she had already seen a similar pattern in the lab. Only two hours ago, she matched it to the other blood on the rounder's bat."

Subliminally something in this description was eating Shakira, but she put it aside for the moment to ask,

"That's a yes then? So the Northern bloke *was* Kenny, and he really *was* in Thorpe rucking with Frazer. Was it self-defence?" She mumbled incredulously trying to process the impact of this revelation.

She looked at both of their faces and yelled as if expressing a sharp pain, "Jesus, do you think Kenny killed Sid as well?"

"Now let's not get ahead of ourselves" Micky responded like someone pulling the reins to slow down a horse. She looked even more confused so Julian added,

"DNA has no timeline, so we are still calculating when he could have left the contribution in the studio" She wondered why Julian had stuttered this, as if betraying a confidence.

"Actually Sid's death was most likely to have been suicide" Micky interjected rescuing him from himself, "but there are just some bits of old squit we will need you to help us clear up."

"Why me? I've hardly seen the man for the last twenty years so I can't give you much of a deposition. Anyway you are beginning to sound suspiciously like Columbo with his 'loose ends'. I presume my biblical knowledge of Kenny was your excuse for continuing my torture, so what was my latest transgression?"

The embarrassed silence hadn't answered the question.

"Alright, let me put it this way what exactly is the nature of this squit?" she said wearily "I have nothing to hide, so let's get on with it so we can all go home"

The effect of what seemed to be a calculated silence, and the muttering amongst themselves, pushed her into something bordering on fury again and despite Julian's previous attempt at gentle narrative, his latter dalliance with repartee had developed a somewhat intrusive nature to it. It seemed to indicate that they still had her under investigation, which was sending her crazy. Struggling to put her finger on what they were still concealing, it occurred to her that her workmates thought she and Rocky were cahoots with Kenny. As Gilbert had put it so poignantly, she was certainly not out of the woods yet.

"You don't think we were his accomplices surely?" she insisted rhetorically.

This thought had caused her to shudder. Micky scotched this immediately,

"No, we don't Shakira, we think Kenny was your stalker"

She shuddered again. Her role in this had jumped from having all the hallmarks of a conspiracy with Kenny, to this sudden bizarre revelation. Her disbelief in their assessment caused her to rebut his assertion with logic,

"No I can't see that. Kenny was just not that into me. He shared a flat with me and my boyfriend for god's sake, he brought loads of women back there. One even remained my lodger after he'd left. It doesn't make sense. I'm not pretending Kenny wasn't off the wall with a distinct Machiavellian side, more than a bit bonkers and a terrible drunk, but I can't see him following me about like a lost puppy, it wasn't his style.

Her scepticism wrong footed Julian so trying to explain his reasoning he changed course slightly,

"Didn't you say he was a bit of a computer geek?"

"I had heard he'd become a bit of a whizz-yes" she recalled "he had been a phone engineer and part of his redundancy package was an advanced IT course. All this was way after he left London"

She was well aware the chronology still confused Julian, but she understood where he had been trying to go with this,

"So you're convinced it was him messing with my computer? What for? Anyway it could have been any old nerd. Let's be honest the force has its own 'white hats' perhaps someone does not like my politics, who knows"

She maintained this inference so adamantly, that she knew it would manipulate Julian into revealing more than he meant to. He was not good at subterfuge, even with guilty ne'er do wells, let alone with Shakira.

"I have a confession to make." he conceded "Kenny has already been linked to a library card used at St Williams Way. He used some kind of phishing technique to bypass all the security. Theirs and ours. There was no trace on the user name, until they uncovered a Nottingham library card with the same false name, with an address very near his sisters'. At first you and Rocky were the only logical connection."

Still asserting her 'innocent suspect' persona she sniped,

"Your logical connection was tenuous, to say the least. Rocky had never met Sid or been to the farm and neither of us have actually been in the studio. The first time I went to the farm was to talk to Anna and Rocky had only ever met Hal once and that was in The Shark's Tooth. In fact I'm beginning to find your earnest testimony a little far-fetched, detectives. Have you actually arrested Kenny? Is he in custody? Do you wish me to make a full statement now, or are you going to suddenly drop the charges?"

Julian said, calmly "Yes, I'm sorry, I should have been more transparent!"

"Yes you should!" she interrupted still seething "and so where is Kenny exactly?"

"They are still trying to find him, he's disappeared and…"

Suddenly there was a knock at the door. It was a solicitor who had been sent by Rocky. Micky apologised to him for wasting his time. As he headed for the door Shakira stopped him,

"Hang on a minute, please. I'm not entirely convinced I don't need a solicitor yet!" realising she was playing to the gallery she added, "Neither of you has given me reason to trust you"

Micky assured her that she had been exonerated but she took the solicitor's card before he left anyway.

"Convincing as you may sound Detective Sergeant Saint" she said "I would have preferred that declaration in writing, and I'm sure Rocky would like a copy too".

Julian promised, "We have already asked him to come in tomorrow, not to interrogate him but for him to assist us in finding Kenny. Straight talking from now on Shakira, I promise, no more intrigue. I absolutely hope you will resume your position with us"

He added tittering "Safely back under Micky's left-wing, of course."

"I'd like that on paper too" she chortled causing Julian to sigh with relief.

The next morning Rocky joined them after nine. He had felt the need to say his piece strongly and his tone intentionally, at least to start with, bordered on a threat,

"We have discussed the situation at length. Despite all the apologies I wasn't sure Shakira should continue working with people who had just wrongly accused her of such a serious crime, especially as she was supposed to be one of their own!"

She was purposely not giving Rocky a chance to finish, just in case, but nevertheless, she felt the need to back him up, addressing Julian testily as if he were still under her scrutiny.

"I had trusted you two with my life and Becky's behaviour, particularly, had been down right treacherous!"

"Since I presume I am still in your employ, unless there are any objections, I would like to resume my research. That is with the proviso that in the future you keep me properly informed and I would like some assurances this time. As for my trust, you have still not earned that"

She was still wary, hurt and frustrated at the injustice she had suffered, but as her exigence subsided Shakira's tone became more obliging. Sensitive to this, Rocky tried not to reiterate his bubbling fury at their duplicity. After a lot of compromise, a new written contract and a plea from Micky for their assistance, they came to an understanding.

Arthur's timely interruption of negotiations was ostensibly to tender his personal apology and to express delight in her decision to continue as an intern. His authoritative figure reminded her that some of her renegade behaviour could have easily landed her in hot water, had there been a less unfortunate circumstance. As he left the room she vowed to quit her protest while she was ahead,

Her undeserved congeniality resulted in a constructive discussion about Kenny's most likely bolthole. Rocky headed off for the school and before they wrapped up, she took a peek at Micky's notes previously not considered for her consumption. Then it began to dawn on her.

Thinking aloud in Julian's general direction she pondered,

"Just because he fooled the barflies in The Eagle that he'd already gone off to the US when he was in fact round the corner, does not mean he is not there now. His mates would not have pulled the idea out of a hat. As soon as Rocky and I arrived, he knew the heat was and he needed to skedaddle. He planned his escapes to include his next destination, and the favourite at this point would have been Oregon!"

"Oh Christ, that makes finding him pretty impossible, even if the I.C.P.O agree his were crimes of 'moral turpitude'" Julian pondered pessimistically spouting legalese.

"I'll see what I can come up with." Micky burbled unconvincingly,

Julian may have been lost somewhere in a medieval dictionary, but he still instructed Micky to contact the Police in Oregon on the quiet. He began wrangling with red tape, and after a week or so he announced,

"I'm afraid we could not corroborate enough proof for extradition, but I sufficiently persuaded the Oregon State Police of Kenny's potentially violent instability. After a lot of to-ing and fro-ing and only as a gesture of reciprocal co-operation, they sent an ICE agent to his room to check his green card application and status. Their mere threat of arrest for an immigration violation, convinced him he should return to Blighty at their expense. Within a couple of weeks he was held by Norwich Airport's Border Controls. We drummed up a reason for them to hold him in custody, they obliged and Micky is about to pick him up."

Unconvinced by his lack of resistance Shakira chuckled,

"You won't hold him long, Kenny's mendacity has made him Houdini, and his ability to slither out of situations with a porky or two, is legendary. What charge were you hoping to hold him on?"

"Actually, at the time we had planned to bring up an old outstanding burglary, but when he saw a couple of officers approach the interview room, he threw a massive fit. While in custody we got him seen by a clinician who shunted him off to some medium secure unit."

"Under the circumstances" she began with genuine concern "and just in case he really does have a problem with Rocky, I would like to be told where they have housed him. Especially if he might be dangerous."

Arthur appeared as usual just at the right time in the conversation to reassure her,

"Kenny has been detained for 28 days pending an assessment and treatment. I am not permitted to disclose the exact location, but I will tell you as much as I can. After all we relied on the testimony from you and your husband to keep him locked up. In the unlikely event that he is bailed, steps have been taken to protect your husband immediately."

Much as the usual 'need-to-know' guff irked Shakira, she was comfortable in the knowledge that Kenny's problems were being dealt with and he was not on the loose. The wheels of Justice turned slowly and they had waited nearly three months before he was actually sitting in the dock.

As the entrance to the Crown Court filled up with people, Rocky and Shakira could not help feeling anxious. Even though they had been through this procedure before and the solicitor had prepared them for every eventuality, they were still not sure how the whole nasty business was going to pan out.

Shakira stood almost oblivious to her surroundings for a moment, contemplating the likelihood that Kenny killed Frazer. Julian had thought the Psychiatric Reports had been thorough, even if they were disappointing inaccurate. Arthur was particularly sceptical about their assertion that Kenny was not much of a threat and that he had been sufficiently medicated.

If it was decided he had been in control of his actions, he would stand trial immediately, probably for manslaughter. She struggled to take in his moral desolation. Whatever his state of mind, his culpability was inexcusable. Julian had expected the solicitor to use his psychological vulnerability to bail him out, but Kenny was having none of it and requested to remain at the facility. Remorse perhaps, she thought, but she doubted it.

Rocky and Shakira were unsettled, confused by assurances that he was not in court today and that they were unlikely to need to testify. While they waited in the public area as the proceedings unfolded, they received more snippets of information. It would seem neither of them had known much about their best mate/former lover. Including the PTSD, that caused him to be discharged from the army.

Then an usher came and advised them that the case had been adjourned, and Kenny had been returned to the secure unit. This time his incarceration was official and mandatory.

During the hearing it had emerged that Jericco and Gilbert were part of the National Crime Agency. Perhaps that was why they had remained lurking in in the wings. They sat with an authoritative looking man whose clandestine note to the judge had secured the outcome. As everyone started to leave this man approached Rocky and Shakira and then accosted them into a side room. When they entered Jericco, already ensconced in the corner with Gilbert, introduced their chaperone as his guv'nor Chief inspector Andrew McIntosh, who requested their "continued assistance if they didn't mind."

Up to this point, Shakira had retained a nagging feeling that the police still thought she and Rocky were somehow partly responsible for his fracas with Frazer. Especially as there was an indication that Frazer's cause of death had opened up a can of worms. Now she realised if Kenny had committed this random act of violence, he was likely to be responsible for other deaths. In fact she knew her knowledge of his character was not as exculpatory as they thought so for once she kept silent and listened.

Usurping his position as her new authority figure 'Andy Mac', his preferred title, began clarifying his plan,

"I have squared it with Julian for you to work with us, retaining your usual salary plus expenses." He turned to Rocky,

"Just for now I would like you to go home to the kids and if possible, to attend the station for a briefing tomorrow morning with Shakira." He smiled in awareness that this 'dutiful spouse' role would normally be a wife's experience.

"In case you have any misgivings I would like to reiterate the assurance that it is Kenny, and Kenny alone we are interested in and he is safely interred."

After Rocky left, he explained to Shakira,

"We understood this case was unlikely to end up running today because of the suspect's fragility. To be honest, most of the inquiry concerning Frazer's death has been all but concluded as self-defence. Despite his state of mind, as long as he has insisted that he is happy to continue talking to us, the powers that be are happy to permit it."

After a pause he asked "How do you and Rocky feel about potentially helping us to encourage a further probe into his mental capacity?"

Shakira was no longer surprised by this possibility or the question.

"There is no love lost between Rocky and Kenny anymore, they irreparably fell out a long while back, and personally I had long since become aware that Kenny's explosion of insanity has made him a danger to himself and other people. Protecting the public is exactly what made me want to join the force in the first place, I assume that answers your question.

"We hoped you would see it that way" he acceded,

"Consequently, although rather unorthodox you will start with us, as soon as Kenny can be made available. Sorting out your security was no problem as he won't know you are present. You will observe Kenny being questioned, through a one-way mirror. Your unique insight into Kenny's character has already moved the case forward immeasurably and I feel your contribution will help us to discover the crucial element that has eluded the CPS so far-his motive!"

The enigma of Kenny's warped reasoning may have eluded the entire police force including the psychologists but not Shakira. She understood him better than most.

Chapter 13 So Close to Murder.

Andy Mac was a dependable, solid sort of policeman. It was fair to say he had the corporate mentality, 'the blue sky thinkers' are so keen on. Not corporate in the domineering way that Arthur presented, but make no mistake, beneath his friendly disposition veiled a scantily cloaked dark spirit, best left under the stairs. That recognised, Shakira found him congenial and erudite, which in a work situation would do for starters.

At Wymondham's Police Investigation Centre, they waited for the van to bring Kenny. Andy began to spitting the odd snippets at her, whetting her appetite for answers, the way her Dad used to when he hid the last two bits of jigsaw. Her expression enticed him to reveal a little more,

"We want you to assist in discovering what role Kenny really played in recent events and why he was so obsessed with tapping into your computer. Usually stalkers want their victims to know they are watching, but it appears he didn't. He just emerged from the undergrowth now and again, like a sort of jinx. We don't know that Kenny had been criminally responsible in other instances, but we need to collate all the gathered intelligence to be certain.

"I'm afraid some of the juicy bits must remain sacrosanct until we are sure we don't need to take him to court. I need not remind you that everything I share with you *must* be sanctioned by the higher ups, and your confidentiality is vital in case we need to prosecute."

"Kenny's psychological problems, theoretically were contained by meds, but his 'trick cyclist' has been looking into some of his more clandestine behaviours prior to his clash with Frazer. She is concerned that his behaviour is not what it seems. Choosing to remain a patient in a secure unit, even as an alternative to remand and asking to be interviewed are unprecedented behaviours. None of his ramblings so far could be used in legal proceedings but recording his 'help with our enquiries' will be useful in any 'fit to plead' decision as long as we maintain a duty of care."

She was painfully familiar with all this legal claptrap but before she could comment, Andy received a message in his ear and flashed a glance at Shakira whilst placing his finger to his lips. She watched through the glass as Kenny was shuffled into the room. His solicitor sat behind him looking disapproving. She supposed the others were medical minders of some ilk.
Kenny exhibited a more dishevelled and unhappy persona than she had ever seen before. His expression was sullen and introverted. This normally eloquent and energetic man, had become a shadow of the talented and vibrant musician she had once been close to. He struggled with his speech and movement and however manipulative he had been and whatever he had done, she could not help a little of her feeling compassion for this genuinely broken man,
Gilbert and Jericco re-introduced themselves to him. After some reasonably pleasant chit-chat Jericco enquired,
"Do you mind talking about why you retracted the statement concerning the injuries Frazer sustained after your conversation at The George, Mr McCann?"
He 'ummed and ahhed' and behaved as if he did not remember. Gilbert gently prompted him.
"Do you remember your original statement?"
Kenny looked vague, so he reminded him helpfully "You told us you had only met Frazer once and only been in The George once."
Kenny jerked his head and shoulders and barked furiously,
"Of course I remember."
Gilbert continued,
"Apart from Frazer's, the only other blood found on the bat was unquestionably yours. We know you argued with him in the pub just before he met his unfortunate end."
Kenny shrugged. Shakira found this line of questioning curious,
"Wasn't he leaving open a plea of self-defence." she whispered "in any case he's being played,"
"He is opening up a dialogue." Andy Mac handed her a copy of Kenny's first statement.
"It is part of a strategy used to build rapport in order to facilitate a proper grilling later, snowflakes permitting. We need to know what his state of mind is."

With an impish grin on his lips he began talking quietly away from the mic almost in mitigation to his last remark,
"At the moment we are only permitted to engage him in gentle discussion. We are attempting to ascertain some logical purpose in his behaviour. Don't fret my girl, as soon as we get a medical green light, Keith and Jamie will crucify him"
"Under caution before he maintained Frazer had insulted his best friend and was spoiling for a fight. Then later he professed he'd never been to a George pub or met a Frazer and his medication was making him say things he did not mean. Later under the bloody doctor he reverted to the original idea, that Frazer started it, Keith is trying to make him decide what porkies today's fairy-tale is going to throw up,"
She nodded and threw her eyes up as if to say "yes, yes" but kept her obedient and respectful silence.
After very little progress, Kenny fidgeted like a child then said he needed the loo. Andy Mac insisted that until he was brought back Shakira should sit tight.
"Remember, he must not know you are here, Shakira"
After they had shuffled him out again and having seen Shakira's bemused expression while shaking her head, Andy was a little taken aback when she quietly voiced with venom,
"It's all an act you know, Kenny's demons might be catching up with him but he doesn't give a shit, one way or another. He has never had a conscience. You asked me here because I know your suspect well. Well for what it's worth, I think he is a psychopathic serial killer who is in the process of constructing some sort of psychological alibi. Andy Mac was so taken aback by her statement, he did not know how to reply so he filled in some more gaps whilst they waited as he thought about it,
"Well recently Frazer's friend at the George picked Kenny out as the man at the bar with Frazer that day. After that Frazer had been seen wobbling around drunk in the garden sporting a bat and The George does not play host to a rounder's team.
"Even if you had considered the possibility that Kenny had acted in self-defence and he has never used that excuse, because he blatantly didn't!" she pointed out

"As this 'taking a turn for the worse' nonsense was after his original statement you can be sure he is twisting you round his little finger."
Andy said,
"But the pathologist had already agreed that even if Kenny did belt Frazer hard enough to finish him off, he had no knowledge of the debilitating effects of the condition of Frazer's liver, so it would be hard to prove he intended to cause his death."
She replied,
"Of course Kenny intended to cause his death. I can't imagine how you can go along with self-defence. I feel like tearing my hair out at the illogical behaviour of a protective force that punishes people on the side of the law like Rocky and I, but wants to excuse a murder machine, because he is smarter than they are!"
Andy Mac did not know how to reply to her unexpected condemnation. Shakira was one step ahead already mulling over Kenny's aspirations for an insanity plea. Her recollections of Frazer's violent temper and fixation on weaponry moved her to point out casually,
"Of course there were tales that Frazer had an automatic pistol which he was also given to waving about and The George does not sport a gun club licence either. Of course owning a shooter may well have been a yarn of Frazer's own invention as we know he was a legend in his own lunchtime, but it would explain why Kenny went to see him, he likes guns and has a penchant for purloining them from idiots"
Missing her point Andy said,
"Do you really think Frazer could have had a pistol, Shakira?"
She was surprised at Andy's reaction, as if this gossip was completely new to him.
"Possibly, but what I meant was that even if he did," she clarified "there was a reason. Why would he have bothered intimidating people with a rounder's bat?" she tried to explain,
"I suppose lots of people in Norfolk own guns, some of them even have guns that are legal," she laughed sarcastically,

"He may have shown it off but if he started waving it about, he'd have ended up spending the night in her Majesty's local B&B. Presumably even Frazer would have been bright enough to have kept it stashed it away. I doubt he had the intention or the guts to use it, and would only have betrayed its whereabouts to someone he hoped would be likely to cough up dollar to buy the thing. He would have been putty in Kenny's hands "
Eventually, Kenny returned, refreshed. He had been virtually carried out of the room but came back under his own steam. This time he was accompanied by a doctor that Shakira already knew, and another woman with a clip-board who Shakira guessed was some calibre of social worker. His solicitor sat quietly in the corner again, nervously biting a pen, making Shakira wonder if he had the burden of some knowledge the police should be party to.
Kenny looked more comfortable now. He started speaking a little more lucidly and confidently, although he remained a pale reflection of the bloke she remembered.
"I have been instructed to explain why I acted in self-defence" he begun as Shakira sucked air through her front teeth in disgust
"You see the man I was talking to, began behaving very drunkenly and started dissing someone I was close to while he was falling all over the place. Then he got nasty, waving this stupid bat around. He hit me a couple of times so naturally I got up and hit him back hard. That's when he fell and bashed his head on the tree and knocked himself out. I thought he was just sauced."
The solicitor smiled at this uncalled for revelation.
At Shakira's suggestion and led by Andy's voice in his earpiece Jericco asked out of the blue,
"Did you ever meet Sid?"
Pretending not to be wrong footed by this change of strategy and the manner in which it was delivered, Kenny replied coolly inferring hindsight,
"I had been in bands with some of The Barbarians, yeah I met Sid a couple of times" he mumbled oozing matter-of-factness.
Jericco asked him, "So did you meet at his farmhouse?"
Avoiding a reply he began raving about Hal instead,

"They all wanted to get rid him you know. I can't see why Sid put up with him, he was a pain"
"You mean Hal was a pain?" Gilbert suggested "you thought the band resented his interference in their PR?"
Kenny's answer made it blatant that he was not interested in anybody's PR in fact PR of any sort, then he suddenly stared at the wall and almost crying said,
"It was because Hal threatened to kill someone I was looking after, he should have been sent down! I told them but they never took any notice"
"Told them what Kenny?" Gilbert spoke suddenly "that Hal should go to prison?"
"Yes, I mean about the threats, I did tell the coppers in the Shark's Tooth"
"Why should he be in prison then?" said Gilbert "You mean because of Sid?"
"Because of the Filofax!" said Kenny as if it was obvious.
"That's why I put it there when I went in to clean up the furniture. I wanted you to find his Filofax and bang him up to stop him hurting anyone."
Jericco looked confused but Shakira had already started putting this together. All the dots were connecting. She had also realised Kenny had been more than just a digital voyeur, where she was concerned. He had sound reasons to study her data. Led by Shakira, Andy whispered into the mic again prompting Jericco to move on again,
"Did you ever meet Ethan?"
"No he was just a friend of a friend" Kenny said dispassionately,
"Who's friend, yours?" said Jericco sounding even more confusing than Kenny.
"Nahh!" he said as if everyone else was stupid again.
"Anyway my mate Nikos told me where they were. I didn't want them upsetting Ethan again. He'd been good to a close friend!"
Just as they seemed to be making some headway Kenny said he wanted to stop and go back to sleep because he felt ill. Although the doctor and social worker concurred Kenny suddenly went on adding,

"It wasn't me who took Ethan's stuff you know it was them stupid scousers. I wanted to teach that bloke Jack a lesson" he whined frustrated at the irrelevance.

"Sorry, you were telling us where you got the Filofax" Jericco said as he tried to rein Kenny in again, while he was still gabbling.

"Look I knew she would go there eventually. At the Francis Drake, it was so easy to tap into her phone I didn't even have to use her Bluetooth."

He laughed triumphantly,

"I followed her to the house and saw my chance. Sid's key was still under the flower pot. They did not come out even though the dogs barked, so I nipped in quick with the Filofax and wiped the furniture."

At this point Kenny slumped on the table as if he was exhausted by his disclosures.

Shakira sensed one of the protective entourage present would finally put a stop to his ravings which had rapidly declined into mussitation.

Although not her intention, her next comment came across to her new colleague almost as if she was excusing her former lover,

"Kenny told me he had learned to be a prolific burglar as a kid, from the necessity of hunger. He had come from a difficult and dysfunctional family. He did not like to talk about his childhood but both me and Rocky assumed it was because it was probably horrendous."

It made Shakira suddenly realise that that day at Anna's he had been within feet of her, too close for comfort. She felt that little shudder again.

As Kenny left, Andy Mac went on to explain to her,

"The techies told me that Kenny's anonymiser failed him that day. The tiny library was so quiet only three people had used that day's pin number. This made it easier to track the false details Kenny had used. He had not realised the implementation of such a simple security measure in a tiny backwater, along with the police's excellent technical support team, would lead straight back to his IP address.

When Shakira got home Rocky asked what sort of mess cranky Kenny was creating now.

"Not much, he would be have been indoors by now doing life if any of them listened, but I think I can throw some light on one of the rozzer's cock ups, but I need to be careful to check it over. You never went to Sid's did you?"

"Absolutely not!" he said with finality "I never even met the man"

"Good!" she said "I can put pay to another of their misguided little theories. I'll explain what I mean after I've spoken to Andy Mac!"

Rocky was used to her being mysterious and just smiled and gave her a patronising.

"Yes dear!"

In the morning she reported to Andy Mac and asked him if she could have a word. Seeing her expression, he took her straight to the privacy of the interview room and inquired gently,

 "What's bothering you Shakira?

"You wanted us involved because we know Kenny well, am I correct?" she queried.

"Yes…so what's your issue?" he replied expecting a more direct beef about previous mistakes,

"I think you have all been barking up the wrong tree. Kenny's motive is simple he's a killer who likes killing. It's how he intends getting away with it that is complex."

"Please elaborate!" he said, genuinely giving her the floor.

"Something was bothering me about the way Julian revealed that Becky had assumed the DNA had belonged to Rocky. Micky intervened just after he had described it as a contribution. It was must have been semen Kenny had returned to eliminate. That fired off Becky's imagination with some idea that Rocky had been playing away with some groupie in Sid's studio. We now know it was Kenny's but it I don't think a woman was there. It brought to mind singer Adam's assertion that years ago, one of the band had a fling with Sid"

Andy nodded in assent,

"At first I thought it was Mary but supposing he meant Kenny?"

"Sorry?" he barked as if he had just started listening,

"You see I don't think it had been me he was stalking at all. I think it was Rocky!"

Andy Mac nearly spat out his morning coffee. Not because her ex-boyfriend was bisexual, or that he might fancy her husband. It was her lift of an eyebrow that made him catch her inference that Rocky might have slept with Kenny as well, and that it would not have bothered her. She smiled knowingly and resumed her train of thought,

"If Sid did kill himself it could have been the result of blackmail. No one has elucidated on whether happily married Sid had a penchant for men, but I can assure you Kenny did. Oh him, I mean he wouldn't have been seen dead in The Foresters, but it was common knowledge amongst his peers. He hid a lot about himself easily."

Answering his shrug she clarified, "Sorry, The Foresters is a prominent gay bar in Nottingham. Even if his behaviour was scopophiliacal, it was more likely he harboured a secret passion for Rocky than me. In addition Kenny often used to excuse his bouts of violence as 'Protecting a friend', usually a man he fancied. It was almost his grooming method, but let's be specific about this Kenny enjoyed being violent and would use any excuse."

At this point Andy got a message in the earpiece.

"I will bear all this in mind. We need to be quiet as they are bringing him in!" Shakira did not think he took her seriously so she decided to drop this piece of contention for the moment. After the clarity he exhibited the day before, Kenny appeared to be asleep, she were not sure if it was the meds or just exhaustion due to his unsettled, nervous state.

"He looks knackered, Andy" she whispered "He is trying to pretend he is not fit to be questioned?

Jericco was obviously thinking the same and glanced at the social worker who was preoccupied, so he asked him,

"Are you OK to carry on, Kenny?" Kenny nodded enthusiastically like a child.

Gilbert gestured to one of the security men who had brought him in, to sit down next to them. He accepted the invitation briefly, and began to prompt Kenny,

"Remember what you told me in the van and I said save it until we get there?"

He started to mutter gibberish as if he was under pressure. The guard got up again and stood by the door behind them. His social worker shook her head, so they tried to cajole him out of his seat to take him back again. Then, out of the blue, and with sudden fluency he stated,

"All that fuss about a dirty smack dealer, he had already got Jonah and he would have had Bernie if I hadn't got in his way!" Before they could go any further he put his head back on his hands and sobbed violently. Andy whispered in Gilbert's earpiece "He's no good to us in that state they had better lift him up and get him back, we'll see how he is later in the day."

"So he's Robin Hood now" Shakira said, "making out he is protecting the young and innocent"

Andy told Shakira "Useful as it would have been as proper evidence, this little outburst gave us licence to insist on another little chinwag with the shrink"

"However, some of his ramblings with Arc, err Sgt Angel in The Shark's Tooth have been explicated." Andy revealed,

"Yes it was Kenny who turned up the next day, spouting off about revenge." Shakira uttered pretending to pay attention, although her mind was puzzling over something else.

Even Andy was babbling on also in his own thoughts,

"Perhaps that was when he started his plot to fit up Hal, even if it was badly executed."

He grinned as he picked up on his unfortunate pun,

Still deliberating she said,

"You know, if previously Darius had been a regular in the Eagle, it's probably where Rocky recalled him from. It's even possible I had clocked him there myself. Kenny's much publicised hatred of class A's could have easily led him to intimidate Darius to shift his operation to another pub. Darius threatening Rocky's mate Bernie and then mouthing off about us could have been all the reason Kenny needed in his warped logic. Darius possibly only knew Bernie by sight, but Kenny knew him well. I can't help thinking about Darius' overdose. It was exactly the kind of retribution Kenny would enjoy"

Encouraging her 'off on a tangent" method of deduction, Andy enquired,

"Tell me what you know about Ethan, Shakira."

"Well by my understanding he was just a nice lad that liked a bit of puff, not really a criminal as such. Nikos, on the other hand *was* a bit of a lad, but Leila insisted he was never as bad as all that. Kenny told a story about Nikos nearly killing a bloke he force fed vodka because he cheated at cards. Now I think of it though Nikos wasn't the gambler, Kenny was, and that sort of caper sounds more like one of Kenny's little tricks."

"So Kenny was a card sharp then?" Andy Mac still seemed sceptical about some of her theories.

"Big time, he used to get himself in hock. Kenny may have been told it was also one of Jack's vices, but Pascal was a better player. Because he had not met either, I could imagine Kenny confusing the sturdier and taller Pascal with Jack. I'm sure Jack was described as the tough guy, but Pascal looked more the part even if, by all accounts he was intrepidly challenged pussy cat.

We know the van that picked up Pascal alone was one Kenny had bought from Nikos. Nikos and his boys all knew Jack well, but Kenny didn't. Pascal might have recognised the van and assumed the driver worked for Nikos who had already settled his differences with the lads". Her train of thought kept wandering off,

"That's enough for today Shakira, you are beginning to look fraught again!" He spoke to Jericco who confirmed that Kenny had been taken back, so he drove Shakira home.

On the way he asked if she would attend a meeting tomorrow. He wanted to run the transcripts of earlier interviews with Kenny past her to see if she could decipher some of the gibberish. When she got home Rocky also remarked she looked tired. She did not pay much attention and as she was deep in thought Rocky left her alone for a while and poured her a stiff drink. She was beginning to put all this together Kenny was not only a psychopathic stalker but a killer and she needed to show them how dangerous he really was.

Suddenly she decided to ask the person who could help her best, Rocky,

"Supposing his obsession was not with me, but with you Rocky." She asked

"I remember you saying when you were mates he used to dress like you almost like a teenage girl with a crush!"
Rocky laughed and said "Who could blame him!" They both laughed, but Shakira was still pensive.
"All this is him you know Shakira, I know he's locked up but you need to convince them he is dangerous."
The next day they met in the ERSOU offices in Cambridge as she had hoped to talk to Andy Mac alone again but found herself being asked to address the meeting. These were not stupid country bumpkins but none of them seemed to see through Kenny's games. Way out of her comfort zone she took the bull by the horns by asking them questions,
"Who do you think actually put Jonathan in hospital?" Taken aback by her directness, Andy explained,
"By your question I presume you have worked it out yourself. Kenny was drinking with some builders in a pub called The Dragon at the time….." he said, beginning the story.
Shakira shuddered when he mentioned the pub, a stones-throw from her front door.
Andy continued "Everyone in there overheard Jonathan slagging off Rocky. Kenny wound up the blokes by saying that Jonathan was a coppers nark. He kept provoking them in the gents pretending Jonathan was bad mouthing them as well. When they went out for a fag Jonathan was already there and asked one of them for a light. All hell broke loose and the pair of them set about him. Jonathan admitted he was drunk but said he did not know the man with them. We identified the builders but Jonathan did not want to press charges. It was Julian who recognised Kenny's description. Once we'd got him in custody Jonathan ID'd him as his assailant. Kenny said the pub was his local, but none of the regulars had seen him in there before".
Shakira shuddered again. It was a scenario typical of his behaviour.
Andy asked her if this related to her theory about Kenny's motive.
"Yes but I would prefer to talk to you later"

She had overheard Gilbert muttering something about a 'fairy-tale' and Shakira was still mulling angrily over the grilling he and his cohort had put her through albeit under instruction. Nevertheless she took the floor again if a little nervously and asked Gilbert directly, and almost accusingly what he thought was Kenny's reason was for hitting Frazer, obviously a sick man, so hard that it caused his demise.
Gilbert replied,
"Don't ask me he's your lunatic friend!" after a look from Andy he remembered he was supposed to be the professional and said more gently. "I think he is a man who can't hold his drink and has some serious anger issues."
"You know Kenny's problems go much deeper than anger issues, but I suppose you think that is an enigma for your experts who you seem to think could not be fooled!" She went on in this vein desperately trying not to upset the apple cart.
After they had left the meeting, Andy started talking to her about one of the interviews with Kenny when he suddenly but briefly mentioned Reggie the builder. Andy thought some of Kenny's information indicated he wrongly thought Reggie was Rocky's nemesis"
This made sense to Shakira who put Andy in the picture,
"When we arrived in Norwich as protected witnesses, the misinformed local grapevine had decided we must be gangsters who had grassed up their mates."
"It might be a bizarre notion but Kenny found lying so easy. Convincing the local chuckleheads that Reggie owed Rocky vast amounts of money would have appealed to his warped perception of an excuse for violence, Reggie was asking to get battered. The trowel would have been his sort of symbolism but he just liked hurting people really"
Before they went Andy spoke less formally,

"These two are good coppers Shakira and experts in procedures, I know the 'all boys together' attitude is wearing, if you feel intimidated I might remind them they can be assigned to another case. I am hoping one day you will make a good detective, so keep with it and don't be fazed by them as they might think you are more resilient than you really are. In the meeting tomorrow back at your own nick I want you to talk about the real Kenny and his real motive!"

She liked the phrase 'own nick' but better she liked the way he subtly endorsed her theory.

The room was packed when she arrived. Everyone she had ever worked with, and many more besides were discussing the case excitedly. Andy's enthusiastic introduction could have been for a cabaret act

"Shakira knows Kenny McCann better than any of us and is going to put forward a line of enquiry I would like us to explore." As she began Arthur left the room to take an urgent phone call, "Kenny liked men as well as women, but his personality was always a lot more complicated. What really turned him on was violence. Let's just suppose for a minute that my husband Rocky was the object of Kenny's desire? Even a psychopath like him could not make sense of that as self-defence. It's just another ploy."

She waited for the shit to hit the fan but there was a wall of stunned silence.

She carried on regardless,

"Let me start with Jonathan in the Dragon. Kenny knew Rocky and I would not drink in the Dragon because of the governor, but his customers knew us really well and I have identified the builders that Kenny was winding up. Instigating brawls in pubs was one of Kenny's favourite pastimes. In London, Kenny would appear as if he had just arrived, just as a fight was breaking out. Actually he had spent hours goading someone in another bar. It was quite likely that two-faced Jonathan was saying things about Rocky that any friend would take exception to!"

Julian did a pretend scowl at Shakira dissing Jonathan who was not in the room to defend himself. She obviously enjoyed getting her own back on the little creep and Julian knew exactly what he was like and he smiled, desperately tried not to show approval.

In support of Shakira but diverting from her opinion of Jonathan, he interrupted briefly
"The psychiatrist commented that she was aware that this little spat may well be pertinent to Kenny's later behaviour."
This subtle endorsement even by a psychiatrist made Shakira feel more confident about her assertions, so she went on to another example,
"Recent exploration by forensics did not uncover or suggest any reason to think that Sid's suicide was anything but that, a suicide, but I am not so sure.
"Whatever we discover it induced Kenny into some interesting behaviour. Kenny had left a contribution of semen in the studio which he tried to remove when he planted the Filofax. Everyone who knew him assumed he was already in Oregon. Actually he was following me from The Francis Drake to Anna's. His purpose being to fit up Hal who he had witnessed threaten Rocky. He had been in Nottingham when Rocky and I were there, probably watching from round the corner. Soon after Darius died in Thorpe. Darius had threatened Rocky"
She could see people around the room, gradually recognising this anecdote's plausibility
"I just want to mention my other visit to London at this point. Edward Albie was my friend who Rocky had never set eyes on until he met me. Of course they have become friends since. I did not know Manny had tried to sell our address, but Kenny used to flit back to Islington often and I am still toying with the idea that he could have said he took retribution to protect Rocky. However surprised he pretended to be the first time in the Eagle he must have already known we were together"
As Shakira paused a still sceptical Micky took the opportunity to interject,
"Why would he hurt Agnes? That was a bit of a coincidence you investigating a case involving your old neighbour wasn't it? Do you think Kenny was the bloke in the ballroom?"
"Yes I do. I have come to believe he is a cold psychopath who killed Agnes to frame Duane. In his warped head anyone who was a threat Rocky was fair game and he intends using that as part of his insanity defence." she said, wondering if anyone was still following all this"

"The only coincidence was my prior encounter with Duane which was obviously why Nick and I were sent to Yarmouth in the first place" she said accusingly whilst pondering the word insubordination.
"As you said Micky there was only ever circumstantial evidence against Duane and with no financial motive this theory is dead in the water, if you will pardon the pun!" she drew breath and then before anyone else spoke Gilbert said,
"Surely his is only food for thought. I just feel we should consider all possibilities" Julian interrupted by scrabbling frantically for something in a cupboard.
"Let her carry on.Is there a problem Julian?" said Andy
"OK Sorry!" he replied.
"Here it is!" said Julian interrupting again by showing Shakira an old photo printed from The Yarmouth Mercury website and saying,
"I meant to show you this earlier. It's a terrible picture but I think that's Kenny isn't it?" he asked Shakira excitedly
"Yes, it looks like him" she said tentatively wondering what he was on about.
"A camper took this on his phone when the trouble started in the ballroom that night and gave it to the paper. So that puts him in at the camp and probably in the pool, we'll need to talk to Duane, as a witness this time!"
Shakira seemed in another world again as she weighed up the situation. She turned to Andy and said something that stopped them all in their tracks,
"Have you used the Holmes2 system on this case?"
"You mean to identify a possible serial killer?" he asked visibly shocked at her earnest belief that Kenny was just that. She nodded in agreement. They were all stunned into silence.
After the meeting Julian requested they all attend an early meeting because Arthur wanted to get a new investigation underway that covered all bases.
During this time Arthur was still on the phone. As they left they could still hear him shouting frantically down the phone at someone through the walls of his office. It was out of character and so impossible to ignore that she asked
"What's all that about?"

"I'm not really sure. He mentioned earlier some issue with wherever Kenny was being kept" Julian said honestly as he walked with her to where Rocky was waiting in the car.
Before picking up the kids they stopped at the supermarket to get something for tea. Rocky parked next to the doctors, not noticing it had become a disabled spot. As they strolled through the shop, talking quietly about her day's events Rocky saw Alistair a nurse from The Norvic Clinic with a couple of his charges in tow. He gave Rocky a smile and that subtle Norfolk nod of recognition.
Rocky had worked at the clinic briefly as a chef and Shakira knew Alistair from the pub, although she did not know where he worked. As they returned to the car, Rocky bleeped the doors opened and had begun loading the boot with shopping. Shakira was still chatting to a neighbour by the shop's back door. Alistair led his charges towards the wooden stairs behind the supermarket, a shortcut to the business park. It had occurred to Rocky that a couple of them were vaguely familiar, even the one at the back who was obscured by hoodie.
Shakira did not really notice his companions, she was busy thinking about how stressful the day had been. As she approached the car, she looked up to wave goodbye to Alistair, vaguely curious about the people behind him. In a split second she recognised one of them. She threw herself on the floor behind the car and shouted,
"Hide, Rocky! That was Kenny!" As she started to dial 999, out of the corner of his eye Rocky spotted something shiny. A pistol was pointing at Shakira.
There was ONE SHOT!

Printed in Great Britain
by Amazon